WORTH THE RISK

Seaside Sisters Series
Book 4

KAY LYONS

Kindred Spirits Publishing

For more information about Kay Lyons, please visit her website at www.kaylyonsauthor.com.

@KayLyonsAuthor (Twitter)

Kay Lyons Author (Facebook)

Author_Kay_Lyons (Instagram)

Kay Lyons, Author (Pinterest)

SIGN UP FOR KAY'S NEWSLETTER AND RECEIVE UPDATES ON NEW RELEASES, CONTESTS, PRE-RELEASE BOOK INFORMATION, EXCLUSIVES AND MORE!

Chapter 1

Frankie Cohen ignored the trembling in her hands as she rolled her Harley Softail Slim to a stop and flipped the kickstand into place. She forced herself to inhale and exhale a timed breath as she cut the engine and removed her old-school helmet. Another breath, counting as she did it. Finally she swung her leg over the seat and winced at the instant pull of muscle and scar tissue in her hip and back. She blamed the pain on too much time spent waiting at the airport and sitting cooped up in economy on the flight back to Wilmington, North Carolina, rather than the fact she'd just logged about a billion jolts of tension during her ride to London's Lattes after catching a glimpse of a man behind the wheel of a large Dodge.

Maybe she should keep riding? Go down to the end of the island and back before seeing anyone in her family, much less her too-perceptive twin?

It wasn't him.

She sucked in another deep breath and put her feet into motion.

It wasn't him—and she needed coffee.

"Hey, you're back," London said.

Frankie had barely stepped inside when her sister spotted her. "I'm back," she repeated, looking around the nearly empty space because it kept her from having to face London.

"Well? Did you have fun? Was it as beautiful as the pictures?"

"Yes." Frankie crossed the floor of the old building, her boots making little noise as she found her usual seat at the bar. "Load me up."

"Really? Full-throttle coffee is not going to help your sleep issues. Despite a week's vacation and traveling, you don't want to go home and crash?"

Frankie glared at her younger-by-thirty-seconds sister and waggled her fingers in a bring-it-on motion. "I have a lot of work to catch up on at the garage and I don't want to wait until Monday."

London frowned in disapproval and Frankie eagle-eyed her sister to make sure London didn't try to gyp her by grabbing the decaf. "So what have I missed? Get me up to date."

"Well, Carolina and Silas are going strong and making plans. They really are kind of adorable."

"Plans?"

"Yeah, she contacted the agency that wanted her to house-sit and convinced them to do a test run of allowing them to house-sit as a family. Silas has to have a background check and all, but if things work out, they may be heading somewhere in Europe over the winter break."

"What about Lucy?" she said, referencing their sister Carolina's boyfriend's daughter.

"She's going with. And already researching places she wants to visit while they're there. That kid's brain—"

"I know, right? Can you imagine being that smart at eight?"

"I can't imagine being that smart now," London said with a shake of her head. "Oh, that reminds me, Lucy and Samuel were asked to present their special school project on the tides again at the school's fall festival."

"Bet Sammy loved that."

"Yeah, but Lucy is excited," she said. "Sammy is

trying hard to get out of it and just wants Lucy to do it all."

London set a large mug in front of Frankie and Frankie took a steadying sip. "Anything else?"

London leaned against the other side of the bar, huddling closer.

"One of us is pregnant."

Frankie had taken another sip and swallowed the wrong way. She started coughing, eyes watering as she struggled to breathe. *"What?"*

London handed Frankie a napkin to wipe her eyes and Frankie stared at her, waiting. "Well, don't keep me in suspense."

London grinned. "Ireland had to come clean and tell Mama about her and Dominic eloping because there's no way she's fitting into that gown come June."

"Wow."

"I know, right?"

"That's fast." Dominic had come to Carolina Cove in May, a year after his first wife's death from cancer, and fallen in love with their eldest sister, Ireland. Five months later, they were not only married but expecting?

"They're over the moon with the news, and even though no one is supposed to know about the baby yet, Ireland couldn't keep the secret from us, of course. But Mama and Daddy don't know yet," she clarified. "Considering Mama's reaction to them getting married so soon and keeping things secret, Ireland didn't want to spring something else on her."

Oh, but when their mother heard the news, Frankie could only imagine the reaction. "Wow," she said again, wondering how two weeks could change so much. "You couldn't have texted me any of this while I was gone?"

"You were supposed to be on a vacation. Well, what counts for *you* as a vacation considering you were still technically working. You needed to relax, not worry about stuff here."

Her working vacation was actually making the delivery of a special project for one of her father's military buddies. She'd rebuilt a classic Harley the man had somehow lucked into and taken it to him in the Florida Keys upon completion. Frankie wasn't sure what, if anything, her father had told the man other than she herself was former military with some mad mechanical skills, but the guy had offered her the use of his oceanfront condo as a bonus. She'd been smart enough to accept after working nonstop on building her business since her medical discharge from the military. "Any shocking news with you, Cooper, and his munchkins?"

London smiled like the woman in love she was and shook her head.

"Nope. He'll be here soon with Rocco to work, and the nanny is taking the twins to the beach today. Oh, my goodness, Bella has fallen in love with octopuses for some reason, but get this— she calls them *yucka*puses! It's the cutest thing ever."

Frankie took another long sip of her coffee, wondering how her single sisters had suddenly found themselves either dating or married to men with kids. Granted, Dominic's kids from his first marriage were in college, so he was the one having a second go-round with Ireland's son, Sammy—and now a baby on the way—but London's boyfriend had adopted his four-year-old twin niece and nephew, and Carolina's boyfriend was a single dad to Lucy. Holland was the only sister left unattached.

Well, and her.

But she had a feeling she would be permanently single. She had plenty of male friends. She tended to get along with everyone, but because of her training as a mechanic, a lot of men found her intimidating, whereas the women looked at her as though she was an alien because of her interests, though they appreciated the fact she wasn't out to rip them off as some garages did when a single woman came to them for help.

Still, she wasn't into dating for the heck of it, and if she wasn't interested in a guy, she didn't want to waste his time or hers, so the problem boiled down to the fact that not a lot of men interested her.

Except him.

"Oh. Customers. Welcome! What can I get you?" London asked the couple who'd entered.

Frankie tuned out, her thoughts returning to the Dodge truck and the flash of the man behind the wheel.

What were the odds that it was him?

Movement caught Frankie's attention across the room, and she leaned back in the stool where she sat, her gaze on the kid standing in the tourist trap section featuring T-shirts, mugs, bumper stickers, and the generally overpriced stuff one picks up while on vacation in Carolina Cove, North Carolina.

A glance at London proved her twin sister was still busy with the couple, so Frankie sipped her oversized cup of black brew and kept an eye on the boy she figured to be around twelve or thirteen given his baby-smooth face and lankiness he had yet to grow into. *Don't do it, kid.*

The boy quickly glanced at London to make sure she wasn't paying him any attention, but he didn't see Frankie watching as he slipped a stuffed animal off of the shelf and into his backpack. *Ah, kid. Way to go lowering my expectations of the future generation.*

While London had some nice T-shirts, stuffed animals, and keepsakes, nothing in the store was worth stealing, but apparently the kid thought differently.

Put it back and I won't break your kneecaps.

Because no one messed with her family—much less her twin sister—without also experiencing the consequences. Was she really going to have to call the cops on the kid?

Sadly, it wouldn't be the first time. Far too many people chose the five-finger discount when it came to shops and stores like those her parents and London owned.

Frankie took another sip and waited out the nervous-looking boy. He wasn't an experienced shoplifter because he was way too obvious. The nervous glances, the lack of smoothness. Besides, common sense said take something from hand or ground level so that you weren't making any atten-tion-grabbing motions for people-watchers like herself to see. But, no, he was a top-shelf thief.

London was still chatting up her patrons, which left Frankie sliding off her seat at the counter to cross the floor and get to the door when the kid tried and failed to nonchalantly head that way. She let him get across the threshold for legalities' sake before she turned to face him and blocked his exit, forcing him to take a step back inside.

"Excuse me."

Well, at least he has some manners.

She stared into the kid's baby blues. When he grew up, he was going to break some hearts, if he wasn't already. "Yes?"

"I need to… I'm leaving."

"So soon?" She gave him a hard stare. "Because I think you forgot something."

"No I didn't."

"Oh, I'm pretty sure you did," she said, watching him pale beneath his summer tan. "Dude, last chance. Did you forget a trip to the cash register?"

A bright red flush began creeping up the boy's neck into his face, replacing the color he'd so recently lost.

The teen made a noise and tried to slip by her, but she sidestepped and blocked him again. "Really, kid? You'd rather I call some friends of mine at the police station so you can explain the lack of receipt to them?"

The kid's eyes widened and he swallowed hard.

"You're crazy."

Frankie sighed, crossing her arms over her front as she waited him out. "Yeah, well, I'll own my crazy, but insulting me isn't the way to get on my good side. Now, I can't be certain if you stole the mermaid or the cat, but either way, I watched you shove several things into that bag of yours." She lifted her chin toward the backpack hanging from his shoulder. "Open it up."

"What? No."

"It's not a problem if you didn't take anything. Right?"

"What's going on?"

London joined them and glanced from Frankie to the kid.

"I'm London. What's your name?"

"I'm not supposed to talk to strangers."

That one left Frankie chuckling. "I'm pretty sure you're not supposed to *steal* either."

"Frankie—"

"Dead to rights, Londy. No question."

"I see," London said, her expression changing to one of dread mixed with resignation. "Well, if that's the case, I suggest you give it back or you pay for whatever it was you took, otherwise I'll call the police."

"I didn't take anything."

"Ah, yet another commandment broken." Frankie didn't budge from her slouch against the door, but when the kid looked confused, she sighed again. "The commandments? From the Bible? You know, the one about not telling lies? It goes with the one about not stealing."

London pulled her cell phone from her apron pocket and when the kid looked her way, she quickly snapped his photo.

"Hey—"

"You get a good one?" Frankie asked.

"Don't I always?" London said. "For all of the problems it causes, social media does come in handy, doesn't it?"

"Kid, it's time to fess up," Frankie told him. "You've been caught, now do the right thing."

"What's your decision?" London punched in 9-1 and left her finger hovering over the final digit. "Are you going to deal with us or the police?"

The kid glared at them before shrugging off the bag and shoving his hand into the opening. Frankie watched as he yanked out a stuffed cat with big plastic eyes. "I so totally would've gone with the dog. He's way cuter," Frankie said to him. "What else you got?"

London took the cat from him, and the kid dove in once more to pull out a hot pink Carolina Cove T-shirt.

"Hmm. Not sure that's your color."

"It's for my girlfriend. For her birthday."

"You'd give your girlfriend stolen presents?" London asked, tsking.

The kid's face heated up again and Frankie shook her head. "Come on, open the bag all the way. Now. No holding back on us."

The kid's shoulders sagged but he reluctantly did as ordered. This time Frankie dove in and pulled out a box with a wave ring and matching necklace. "You really went for it, kid. Jewelry, cloth-ing, *and* a stuffie. Anything else?"

"No. I was only going to take one thing but I didn't know what she'd like."

"Well, I'm pretty sure she'd like it better if it wasn't stolen," London said.

"Definitely." Frankie tilted her head and noted

that the kid looked on the verge of tears. Because of embarrassment? Anger? Or part of the innocent act? She honestly wasn't sure. "Londy, how much is all of that added up?"

"Uh, I don't know. Let's see." London did a quick calculation and stated the total.

"Is this the first time you've done this?" Frankie asked. "Or are you a regular visitor in juvie?"

"I haven't… I didn't… I just wanted to get her something nice and I didn't have enough money. We only just started dating and—"

"And you wanted to shower her with stolen gifts." Frankie grimaced. "Way to make an impression, kid."

A shrug was his response, but Frankie noted he did look a little embarrassed by her observation.

"Look, any girl worth impressing wouldn't want something you've stolen. She'd understand you needing to earn the money for a gift."

"But I'm a kid."

"Who is what? Thirteen?" Frankie guessed.

"You have to be sixteen to get a job here," he said, sidestepping the question.

"Not necessarily. You could help clean up yards for your neighbors, walk some dogs, or wash dishes in a restaurant kitchen. You don't need to be older to do those types of things."

"That's what my dad said. But there's still not enough time before her party and… I didn't want to show up and not have anything."

"All I'm hearing are excuses. Where's your integrity?" Frankie watched as the kid shrugged. She resisted the urge to roll her eyes and exhaled. "When's this party?"

"Saturday night."

"And you say you have no time," she said, scoffing. "That gives you two whole days."

"To make that much?"

London exchanged a glance with Frankie and she prayed her sister didn't regret whatever it was she was about to say given the look on London's face.

"If you work hard, yes," London said. "So this is what you're going to do. You're going to come to work for me tomorrow after school, and *all day* Saturday, and I'll cover the cost of the things you tried to lift—or I can call the police."

"Sounds fair to me," Frankie said.

"If you accept, I'll even wrap up the things you chose all nice and make them pretty—once you actually pay for them."

The kid's head swung back and forth between the two of them like he wasn't sure what to make of the offer.

"What'll I have to do?"

Frankie smirked. "Whatever the boss wants you to do. But you don't show tomorrow, then that photo goes to the police and hits social media so everyone in the area knows to be on the lookout for you. Oh, and look right up there," she said, pointing. The kid followed her pointing finger and she watched as he swallowed hard again. "Ah, there's another nice photo for the cameras."

The kid's expression revealed his fear as well as his utter lack of enthusiasm, but after a long moment, he shrugged. "Whatever. I guess I'll do it."

"Smart decision." With his backpack free of stolen merchandise, the kid shifted to the side to try to get by Frankie once again. "Hold up."

"I don't have anything else."

"Yeah, but you forgot something."

When the kid stared at her blankly, she sighed. She hated to sound old but... kids these days. "Don't you think you ought to apologize and thank London for not calling the cops?"

"I'm sorry," he said to London.

"Really, kid? *That's* the best you can do?"

The teen fisted his hands and inhaled.

"I'm sorry I tried to steal your stuff. It was wrong. I should've paid for it and... I won't do it again."

"Now that's an apology," Frankie told him, nodding in approval.

"Apology accepted," London said. "What's your name?"

Another long pause. Frankie could practically see the kid trying to quickly think up a fake one.

"Joey."

Frankie narrowed her gaze on him and really hoped the kid surprised her by showing up.

"Well, Joey, make sure it's okay with your parents first, but be here immediately after school tomorrow. Don't be late."

"It's just me and my dad. He won't care. He'll be happy to be rid of me."

Frankie wasn't sure what to make of that comment, but if true, it could explain some things. "Make sure it's okay, anyway," she ordered. The last thing London needed was an irate helicopter parent breathing down her neck when they'd tried to help the kid by *not* calling the police.

"Can I go now?"

"Sure. Go ahead."

Frankie and London watched as Joey ducked out the door as fast as he was able to get by her.

"Should I follow him?" Frankie asked, though the question was more rhetorical.

"No. Let him be. You brought him down a notch or two. Maybe the experience of getting caught will sway any future plans to do it again."

Frankie traced London's steps back to the counter. Her sister placed Joey's selection in a bag for safekeeping and hung the bag on the door leading to London's apartment upstairs. No doubt so she could wrap and make it pretty like she'd promised. London was such a softie.

"Do you think he'll show up tomorrow?"

Frankie shrugged. "Maybe. It's a toss-up. But if you run out of things for him to do, I'm sure I can come up with a few odd jobs. I can't have him actually working *in* the garage due to labor laws, but between taking out the trash and cleaning the floors and bathrooms, he'd be busy."

"Well, Sammy'll certainly be happy he won't have to pitch in here tomorrow. Ireland mentioned Dominic spent the week in Atlanta, so they'll want to spend as much time as they can with him this weekend."

Sammy was kept very busy working little odd

jobs between the entirety of family-owned businesses, and as such it kept him—mostly—out of trouble. Summer months were always harder, but with an entire family full of people willing to watch Sammy, however, the kid couldn't get away with too awfully much. Unlike Joey, from the sounds of it.

"Just keep him away from the goods," Frankie said with a tilt of her head toward that side of the room. "And the cash register." She settled in on a stool at the bar. Now that the excitement of the petty thief was gone, London talked about her plans for Ireland's upcoming engagement party. While her sister went on and on about food options and decorations, Frankie's mind drifted.

"Helllllo?"

Frankie blinked. "Sorry, what?"

"What's wrong?"

"Nothing."

"Uh-huh. By the way, don't think I didn't catch you acting weird when you first got here. You looked like you'd seen a ghost when you came in. I was too busy with orders to corner you then, but now? Spill."

Shoved back to the event leading up to her making an impromptu coffee run and twin shrink session in the first place, Frankie shuddered at her now cold coffee and silently begged for a fresh cup.

"Fine. Hand it over. And talk. What happened?"

"It's nothing." It had to be nothing. Because it couldn't happen again.

Right?

"That may work with the other sisters but they don't have my twinsie-senses. You might as well tell me what's going on because you're not leaving until you do."

Frankie tapped her fingers against the countertop, wondering how—where—to even begin when the telling spanned… continents.

"It's *that* big of a thing? Frankie, don't keep me in suspense."

"It's not… It's just… It's *weird*."

"Go on."

Frankie inhaled and met her twin's gaze. "Okay, fine. But if you laugh at me or make some kind of snarky comment, remember I've been trained to kill."

London cocked an eyebrow high. "Tell me before I kill you."

"Fine. But first answer something."

"Anything."

"Do you believe in fate?"

Chapter 2

London stared at Frankie like she had two heads.

"Fate? Seriously?"

Frankie sat back in the barstool and glared at her sister. "Do you want me to tell you or not?"

"I do! I totally do. I'm sorry," she said, waving a hand in front of her face like she waved away an irritating fly. "It's just a surprise to hear that question coming from *you*."

"Forget it."

"No, don't you dare. You know what I mean. Of all of us, you're the last one to ever be girly-romantic about such things."

"Fine. Don't call it fate. What about coincidence? Like, *hard-core* coincidence. Do you believe in that?"

London took hold of her long braid and whipped it over her shoulder like she tossed back a cape.

"I believe there is a plan for each of us and things have a way of happening when they're supposed to, so, yeah, I do. Why are you asking? Where is this coming from?"

"It's… Something weird happened today.

"And…?"

London gave Frankie a fresh cup of brew and then placed her elbows on the counter, leaning forward toward Frankie and giving her all of her attention.

"I thought… I thought I saw someone I know—knew."

"How does that equate to… fate? Come on, either fill me in or I'll call the sisterhood, because I *have* to know where this is going."

Calling the remaining three sisters meant heading down to the beach to their special place by the dream catcher mailbox and explaining this to *all* of them. Not something she wanted to do. It was hard enough explaining this to her twin. "No meeting. And this stays between us."

London nodded immediately but her frown revealed her concern.

"Okay. But for the love of coffee, just hurry up and tell me already."

Frankie smiled at her sister's words, but just as quickly, the smile faded and she searched for the right way to tell the story. "When I enlisted in the Marines, I met this guy. And ever since then, everywhere I go, eventually, we… wind up finding each other."

"Like he's *stalking* you?"

Frankie shook her head, hands gripping the warm coffee mug tight so London wouldn't realize how badly they shook. Was she about to see him again? "No. Nothing like that. It's like… life just keeps bringing us back together."

"Thus the question of fate."

Once more she nodded. "I don't even know if it was him, but given our history… It rattled me."

"Why? What happened between you? Do you want it to be him?"

"No." She shook her head to emphasize the word and hated herself for the fear surging to the surface. The anger.

The heartbreak.

"That was an awfully quick response, but it wasn't all that convincing. Are you sure?"

Frankie opened her mouth to confirm her words

but nothing would form. Maybe because, if she were honest, the real reason was because she didn't know if she could stand seeing him again. There came a point in life when a person couldn't handle any more pain. "Just forget it. I have to go. I need to head to the garage."

"Frankie… stop. *Talk* to me."

"I don't know what to say."

"How did you meet? I know you said the Marines, but where? What happened between the two of you that's got you so… freaked out?"

Basics. Yeah, she could do basic questions. And then, maybe, more. "I met him for the first time in boot camp. He was stationed there. And since it was boot camp and I was just trying to survive, it wasn't a big deal. We said hello, ran into each other a few times around the base, and that was it. Then two years into my stint, I turned the corner when I was stationed in California, and there he was again."

"And?"

"And we talked. Flirted a little. Same thing happened in Germany. Then I was sent to Japan."

"I get the sense that's not the end of it. Did you email? Text?"

"No. Maybe I should've known something was up then because he didn't ask for my info."

"You weren't in Japan long."

"No. About a year. Then they sent me to Kabul. And two months later, there he was."

"Wow."

"I know. It's like there's some kind of magnet that keeps pulling us to the same places."

"And there's no way he could have manipulated the circumstances leading up to all of those meetings?"

"No. He didn't have the rank to do that. And even if he did, it wasn't… like that."

"But you think the guy you saw is him?"

Frankie shrugged. "Given the number of times it's happened in the past, maybe. Wouldn't you?"

"I suppose. Even if he couldn't have pulled strings to find you in the past, that doesn't mean he didn't search for you online and track you down."

"He hasn't sought me out, Londy."

"Then why does the possible sight of him have you shaking in your boots? Frankie, if you like this guy, barring the obvious stalker scenario, what's the problem with seeing him again? What are you *not* saying?"

The answers to those questions weren't basic at all. Frankie stared into her cup, unable to find the words.

"Oh, Frankie, is this about your injuries? That won't matter to him. Not if he cares for you, if he's the one for you and all of the coincidences are part of something bigger. Right?"

Heat prickled her eyes and Frankie blinked hard to relieve the pressure. "I don't think your 'something bigger' works in this scenario."

"Why do you say that?"

Frankie felt as though the duct tape holding her heart together ripped off in painful yanks. "Because… after we kept meeting up and hanging out, and after we were able to actually spend quality time together in Kabul and I fell in love with him, I… found out he was married."

London's hands surrounded Frankie's wrists, and when she was finally able to meet her twin's gaze, she saw the love she knew would be there, but also anger.

"Married men should have to have brands on their freaking foreheads or something."

"Some women wouldn't care."

"But good women do and God doesn't send any woman someone else's husband. You wouldn't have allowed yourself to get close to a married man had you known. I'm sure of that."

Frankie nodded because it was true. She'd had

no idea, and the sight of a ring was an automatic hands-off to her. What had started off as simple conversations over the way they kept running into each other had turned into evenings spent playing pool or darts or just talking over a drink with friends. The first few meet-ups hadn't lasted long enough nor had she known him well enough to have been given such personal information being that they were purely random, but later... when they met up *again* in Kabul... In all the hours and all the talking, he'd never mentioned having a wife. "We didn't do anything. We... We almost kissed... It would've been our first kiss, but then he pulled away and said he had to tell me something. I have to give him credit for that. I'm grateful that he stopped, at least, but—"

"But it was too late because you'd already fallen for him."

Frankie nodded, hard as it was to admit.

"What happened when he told you?"

"I flipped. Like, off the rails flipped. I'm not stupid and he could've told me earlier. Like you said, I wouldn't have let myself get close to him *at all* had I known he was married."

"So what did he say?"

Wry laughter emerged from her chest. "He said

it was 'complicated' and something about getting a divorce, but at that point I didn't care anymore. For all I knew, he was lying about that, too. I told him to get lost, which was easy since he was heading back to the States the next day anyway. That's… when I volunteered to cover Muldoon."

"You mean it's *his* fault you were almost killed? Oh, I hope it *is* him so I can—"

"Londy, I didn't want to be there when Grayson left."

"That doesn't matter."

"It does. I *volunteered*."

"And barely lived to tell the tale."

"Even if Grayson *hadn't* been leaving… I would've covered for Muldoon anyway. Just to get some distance. I needed the head space after coming so close to… being the other woman." There was no excuse for cheating. Ever. And any woman who actively pursued a man *knowing* he was married?

Not someone she'd ever allow herself to be.

"You really were in love with him, weren't you?"

Frankie looked into the coffee mug again because she couldn't hold London's gaze. Being one of five sisters wasn't easy. Being the most athletic, rough-and-tumble tomboy of the bunch also meant being considered the toughest, physically and emotionally, and made conversations like this one all the harder to have. In love with him? It was like saying there was a drop of water in the ocean. "Yeah."

Men tended to steer clear of strong women, and she was strong, no doubt about it. But when she'd finally let the barriers down and allowed herself to fall...

Grayson had shattered her with his announcement. And while she knew she wasn't the only woman to ever have her heart broken, it had certainly seemed like she was, and she felt all the more foolish because of it.

Volunteering to cover Muldoon gave her purpose and forced her to focus on something other than the heartbreak. Then again, once the IED blew, everything hurt. She'd never forget that kind of pain. Or the emotional devastation that came afterward when she was lucid enough to learn the full extent of the damage done to her by the blast.

"Frankie?"

"I can't see him again, Londy. It's impossible for fate or th-the plan you're talking about to put us together *again*, right? Because if that's the case, it's *cruel*."

London stared at her but didn't offer any encouragement to the contrary. Maybe because London knew, in the moment, the words would be useless. "I have to go. Can I get one of those to go?"

"Of course." London hurried to grab a coffeepot and fill the request. "Listen…"

"I'm okay. I just got spooked for a second because I'm so tired, that's all. What are the odds, right? No big deal."

London set the to-go cup in front of her and then grasped Frankie's hand in hers.

"Right. And if the guy you saw is him? You've got this. Girl, you survived *war*. You can handle a man. Especially one who has already lied to you."

Chapter 3

Grayson Carter opened the door of their house, tucked back on the southern corner of the island on a quiet street near Ft. Fisher, before his stepson's foot hit the top tread of the stairs. "Where have you been?"

"Out."

"For four hours? Out where? Doing what?"

"Geez."

Grayson followed Christopher to the kitchen and watched as the boy dumped his book bag on the floor by the island on his way to the fridge. "Chris, where did you go after school? Aunt Mary said you didn't show up like you were supposed to."

"Because I had stuff to do."

When Grayson glared at him, Christopher rolled his eyes.

"I rode my bike to some stores to look for something for Cat's birthday. It took a while."

"You didn't answer calls or texts. We've talked about this."

"My phone went dead. What's to eat? I'm hungry."

Grayson battled his temper and reminded himself to be patient. Christopher had been through a lot and it would take time to adjust. "I thought I'd order something. Did you find a present for your friend?"

Christopher still had his head buried in the fridge.

"Yeah, maybe. I don't know yet."

"I'm sure she'll like whatever you get her."

Chris released a grunt and pulled out some string cheese.

"What do you want for dinner? I held off because you weren't home and I'm really not in the mood to cook. Pizza?"

"Yeah. Can we get pineapple, like Mom always did?"

"Sure." Pineapple could be picked off, after all, and battles had to be picked just as carefully. "Get to work on cleaning up your room and I'll place the order."

"But I just got home."

"You were supposed to do it two days ago and now you can't see the floor. Clean your room or you won't be going to your friend's birthday party this weekend."

Christopher grabbed a water bottle from the fridge and slammed the door. He grabbed his back-pack from the floor and headed toward the hallway leading to the stairs.

"Wait," Gray said, "how are you paying for this present?"

"I got it covered."

"Where'd you get the money?"

"Birthdays and stuff. The usual."

"You told me you'd spent all of your cash the last time you asked me for some."

"I forgot about some I'd stashed."

Gray bit back a comment and grabbed his cell from where he'd set it earlier. Pizza. He needed to focus on pizza. Disgusting, pineapple-laden pizza. Not on Chris's questionable behavior and memory.

Had he been as evasive at that age?

Gray finally placed the order and hoped for the best. He had the makings for a salad. Christopher would protest the need for it, but Grayson would do anything to prolong the meal and get a chance to talk. Maybe he could come up with a dessert of some kind. The kid used to love ice cream. Was that still the case? Ever since Grayson had left the military to be a full-time father, the kid had fought him at every turn. Up was down, green was blue, and nothing he ever said or did was right.

The doorbell rang and he frowned, glancing at his cell to check the time. That couldn't be the pizza, could it?

"I got it," Christopher called. The kid scrambled down the stairs as fast as his feet could carry him.

Grayson got up and hurried toward the door, where Christopher stood with a young girl who looked at Gray like he had two heads. "Who's this?"

"Cat, my girlfriend. We're going to go for a walk to the pier."

"Christopher, I just ordered pizza. And you have a room to clean."

Christopher practically shoved the girl out the door, and short of grabbing the kid and forcing him back into the house, Grayson was at a loss.

"I'll be back in a while."

"Be back by eight," Gray bit out as the two rushed down the stairs. "*Christopher*!"

"Whatever," Christopher said by way of acknowledgment.

Grayson watched them until they turned the corner and walked out of sight before he stalked back into the house and slammed the door.

Of all days to get into a fight with his son, why this one? He'd had a long day at work, and on the way home, he'd met a woman on a motorcycle who'd looked—

He swiped his hand over his face again. It wasn't her. And besides, she'd worn a helmet, aviators, and a jacket, so he hadn't been able to see that much of her to identify her.

It couldn't have been her.

Because if the woman was Frankie Cohen, his life was going to get a lot more complicated than it already was.

LATER THAT SAME EVENING, Frankie entered Ace's Garage to make her way to the office and was greeted by a familiar furry face. "Tank! Hey, boy! Oh, I've missed you."

The German shepherd alternated between

wagging and sitting to give her his paw, tongue hanging in a huge smile.

"Hey, Frankie. Welcome back."

"Hey." She looked up to see her mechanic and dog-sitter smiling at her. "Thanks. It's good to be back," she said, straightening to move deeper into the office. She dropped her keys onto her desk and looked at the mound of paperwork awaiting her. That's what she got for a week away on a paid vacation. She'd pay for it, all right. And be playing catch-up for a while. But that white sand and insanely blue water had gone a long way toward lowering her angst factor. Well, until the drive to London's.

"You said to leave it, so we did."

"It's all good."

"Hey, anytime you want to give up a paid delivery to the Keys that comes with free room and board, you let me know," Steve said. "I'll be happy to sub for you."

She grinned at him and shook her head. "No way. That condo and view definitely qualified as one of the perks of being boss."

Tank moved to the bottom of the love seat across the office and hesitated as he prepped to jump. "Did you give him his meds?"

"Yeah, but the poor boy's feeling achy today. Tough for an old man to keep up running around with my crew."

Tank was a MWD—military working dog—retired from bomb sniffing. He'd served eleven years before being placed for adoption after he was injured in the blast that had killed Tank's handler.

Frankie moved to the love seat where Tank was now settled and stared into his beautiful eyes while stroking his head, the ache in her side pulling from her own now-healed injuries. "We'll head home soon," she told Tank softly. The shepherd blinked at her and lowered his head atop his paws with a loud sigh as though content now that she was home.

"Did you have any issues getting down there?"

She shoved herself up from the couch and returned to the desk. "Had to stop and make a few tweaks but nothing major. I took my time and just enjoyed the ride. Jerry was a happy camper. He couldn't wait to show it off," she said, referring to the Harley she'd spent the last several months restoring. "What are you still doing here? You could've left Tank at the condo. You fishing for overtime for your trip?"

"Nah. Just hanging around to give you the good news."

"Oh? Must be good."

"It is. A miracle walked in today. Been killing me keeping quiet until you got around to showing up."

"A miracle, you say?" She sent the man a suspicious stare and paused in the act of sorting way too much mail. "Well, I'm intrigued. Fill me in."

The Gulf War vet grinned and bounced on the flippers that made up the feet of the double prosthetics appearing out from beneath the shorts he wore.

"Remember that beehive taillight you've been searching high and low for?"

"No way."

"Yeah. Had a kid come in wanting to sell one today."

Her suspicious nature immediately reared its ugly head, and the joy she'd felt at finally getting a much-needed part for *her* special project burst like a balloon. "A kid?"

"Yeah. About fifteen or so, I'm guessing. Said his old man is a vet, sick with cancer, and needed the cash. Said he'd heard this was a good place to try because of you hiring vets. Anyway, seeing as how you've been looking for one for so long, I bought it. Got a heck of a deal, too."

For the first time since entering the office, she spotted the box propped between the seat and cushion of the chair across from her desk. "Are you sure it's not stolen?"

Steve grimaced but then shrugged.

"Guess there's always a chance of that, but the kid seemed sincere. Been looking online and through the ads since he left while I waited on you to show, but I haven't found anything reported. I'll let you know if I see something."

She set the mail aside to round her desk and check the box over but didn't see anything on the outside. "You get his number or anything?"

Steve grimaced. "No, sorry. He said his dad might sell more parts and tools to pay for bills, though, so he could be back in."

Tools were pricey, and having briefly employed a thief, she was now having to replace tools that had gone missing during the guy's short employment with her. "Gimme a heads-up if he does, and be sure to get some info off of him. How much did he sell it for?"

"Three hundred."

She exhaled with a small whistle as she lifted the taillight from the packing paper and looked it over. "Too good to be true," she said sadly, knowing in her gut she couldn't get too attached to the part because it would probably have to go back to its original buyer. "Thanks, Steve. I appreciate it, but don't buy anything else from this kid until I meet him. I want to check out the story and know he's legit."

"No problem. I figured you would but I wanted to pick that cherry while I had the chance."

She put the part back in the packaging. "Oh, yeah, I'm glad you did. If it's not stolen, it's definitely a find. Thanks for looking out for me."

"You know it," he said with a nod. "I'm going to head out now. You have a good night. Lisa's raring to get on the road bright and early tomorrow, so I need to pack up the van tonight."

"Safe travels. Oh, and lock down the bay doors on your way out, would you?"

"Sure thing. Good to have you back, boss."

Frankie sat in her office chair and went over the schedule for tomorrow before tackling the mail again and perusing the numbers. Time and again, however, her gaze settled on the box across the desk from her. She got up and garnered Tank's attention. The dog watched as she lifted the box onto the desk once more. Maybe there was no label on the outside, but packing slips were sometimes placed inside as well to help derail shipping mishaps. It was worth a shot to hunt for one in case the kid was careless in his attempt for fast cash.

Frankie set the taillight aside and dug around. Just when she was about to give up hope, she spotted a barely visible white tip and pulled it from under one of the box folds.

And there it was. The part had been shipped to—

Her legs gave out and she collapsed onto the edge of the desk.

G. Carter.

She stared down at the slip, Steve's words about the kid's dad being a vet who had cancer sliding through her head, piercing her heart.

Could it be?

She gripped the slip in her fist and fought to breathe as Tank whined and left the couch to come to her side. She buried her fingers into his fur and tried to ground herself in the moment. Breathe. Something to keep from losing herself to the panic swarming her senses.

It couldn't be him.

Hadn't she already lost enough?

Chapter 4

Grayson paced the kitchen in his frustration with Christopher before going back to the living room. He was ten minutes into an '80s sitcom when the doorbell rang again and his stomach growled as if on cue.

Once more he made his way to the entry, digging his wallet out of his rear pocket as he opened the door to tip for a pizza he didn't want for a kid who wouldn't be grateful. A gasp caught his attention and he lifted his head to lock gazes with…

"Frankie?"

She shook her dark head, an incredulous huff leaving her chest as she shoved a box toward him. He dropped his wallet in his effort to secure the box and stared, pulse racing in his veins as she turned without a word and headed toward the stairs. "Frankie, wait. Frankie!"

He tossed the box onto the closest outdoor chair and chased after her, grasping her arm gently to stop her.

A dog began barking and jumped out of an old Jeep, racing toward them.

"You wanna keep that hand, you'd better let go."

He released her immediately and stepped back from the growling dog at her side. "Just… wait a second, okay? Who's your friend?"

"Tank. And why should I wait? The wifey-poo not home to see you flirting with me, so you feel safe?"

He bit back a curse and fought to control his temper. She wouldn't listen a year and a half ago either, but this time… "No, she's—"

"You're *unbelievable*."

The dog's growls got louder, but it didn't move from its spot at her side, even when she lowered her hand to its head.

"She's *dead*, Frankie." Maybe it was a cheap shot by way of insensitivity, but he had to say something to slow her down before she disappeared like she had last time.

He held her gaze, flummoxed like he always was every time he came into contact with her. She was thinner than he remembered but just as beautiful as ever. Her dark brown hair was pulled back from her face in a pony, and unlike earlier today when he'd seen her—if it had been her—she now wore standard-issue olive green shorts and a camo T-shirt.

"Should I give my condolences or congratulate you? I'm a little confused."

And angry. He tilted his head toward the door. "Want to come in?"

"No."

"Will you come in?" he asked next. "I'd like to talk to you and I'd rather not have this discussion in front of my neighbors."

"What are you *doing* here, Grayson?"

A smile pulled at the corners of his lips despite the seriousness of her expression. He shook his head and glanced at the box she'd brought with her. Wait, was that his— "I could ask you the same thing. Where did you get that?"

"Apparently a kid brought it to my garage today to sell. Said his dad was a sick vet with cancer and needed the money."

Christopher. Grayson fisted his hands and his

anger must have radiated off of him, because Tank released another warning growl.

"Your dog has issues."

"He's a retired WMD and he doesn't like it when people yell at me."

"I didn't yell at you."

"I guess he just doesn't like you then."

"What did the kid look like?" It was a stupid question since he was pretty sure those types of parts weren't just lying around in garages at the beach, but asking the question bought him some time.

"I didn't see him. One of my mechanics made the deal. Got it for less than half price, so I figured something was fishy. He'd overlooked a packing slip inside. So is it true?"

He blinked at her, not following.

"Do you have cancer?"

Would she care if he did? "No. What I have is apparently a kid who can't seem to stay out of trouble."

Frankie's expression didn't reveal much, but he knew her well enough to know she was as blown away by their reunion as he was. "It's a little weird how we keep winding up together, isn't it?"

A low huff left her ample chest.

"We're not together. And you didn't answer my question. What *are* you doing here?"

"I'm out. I'm a full-time dad working at a local doctor's office and clinic as their PA."

He watched her close her eyes and fist her hands. Apparently she'd hoped he was just visiting? "Frankie—"

"You knew I lived here. *I* was honest and told you about my life. About my home, my family. Where I lived. You didn't think we'd run into each other? That it'd be a problem for you to be here?"

He ignored the shot at his character, because it was deserved, and took a step closer. "Wilmington isn't some Podunk town, Frankie. Toss in the population of the beaches… Okay, yeah, I'd be lying if I said it hadn't crossed my mind that I *might* see you at some point, but we also could've lived here all of our lives and never run into each other."

"How long have you been here?"

He inhaled. "Since April." And it had taken everything inside of him not to track her down any way he possibly could. Through buddies still in the military, through the internet. But given their history, starting a new job, and his rocky relationship with Christopher, Gray knew he'd needed time to settle in. Get his life on an even keel before anything else.

An exasperated huff left her again.

"Frankie… come inside. Please. Let's talk. Let me finally explain."

She squared her shoulders, lifted her chin, one-hundred-percent pissed female ready to do battle. Her expression changed and he kicked himself for the millionth time for not being honest with her from the beginning.

"There's nothing you can say to explain away the lies," she said before purposefully moving down the stairs like insurgents were hot on her heels.

He took a step, going to follow her, but Tank went up on all fours and growled again. "You and I are gonna have to come to terms," he said to the dog.

"Not happening," Frankie called over her shoulder as she reached the bottom step. "But I am glad you don't have cancer."

He watched her go, taking in every sway of her hips and every bounce of her pony. The long, tanned length of her legs and the proud tilt of her head. She got into an old Jeep that gave off an impressive roar when she twisted the key.

Now that his master was safe, Tank took off down the stairs and leaped into the Jeep beside her, sitting tall and proud on the passenger seat.

Grayson couldn't help the small smile that pulled at his lips at the image they made, all rough and tough and protective of one another. But he knew both had a softer side. He'd seen Frankie's and wanted to see it again.

She might hate him, but she was glad he didn't have cancer.

It was a start and he'd take it. And now that she'd made contact and he knew how to find her... he had some making up to do.

TWENTY MINUTES after Frankie got home, she forced herself to stop pacing and unlock her aching jaw. Her plan had been to stay at the garage to get caught up, but after taking the part to the address on the slip and seeing Grayson face-to-face, she'd retreated to the safety of her home.

Because he was here. In Carolina Cove.

And single because of a dead wife?

She shook her head and groaned aloud. Single or married, it didn't matter. Not anymore. It was too late to undo the damage caused by his lies.

A low whine and the clang of the food bowl jerked her out of her daze. She turned to see Tank staring at her with his big dark eyes and glanced at the time. "Chow time, huh? Steve said you were being persnickety while I was gone. You know you have to eat so you can take your meds."

She got his food prepped and set the bowl back on the floor, filled his empty water dish since Steve had kept Tank at his house rather than here, and looked at her tiny condo. After being in the military, she'd come out with a duffle of clothes and little else. Tank was a new addition, adopted six months after her discharge. The moment she'd read about his PTSD and how he'd mourned his handler, she'd known the dog would understand her hang-ups. Who better to adopt him than someone who understood what he'd been through?

She opened the fridge but didn't see much other than cheese and a bottle of wine. A search for crackers left her taste-testing a hastily twisted sleeve shoved to the back of the cabinet, but they'd gone stale.

Popcorn?

She opened another cabinet and spied the microwavable box kind. One packet left. While the popcorn popped, she poured some wine. "You know, you should learn how to grocery shop to earn your keep."

Tank let out another whine behind her and she glanced back to see the bowl of food untouched in front of him. "What's up with you? I know you're hungry. You never eat much when I'm gone, so have at it."

Tank's eyes flicked from her to the food and back to her with another low, pitiful whine.

"Oh, no," she said, shaking her head firmly. "You're not going to con me into doing that, so don't give me those puppy eyes. I only did that a few times because you were sick after your surgeries, and now every time I go somewhere and have to leave you for a few days, you try to guilt me. What kind of best friend are you? I mean, yeah, you were pretty cool when you came to my defense when Gray grabbed me, but that doesn't mean I'm going to do what you want. When you get hungry enough, you'll eat."

Tank inhaled a shuddering breath and sighed, the sound emerging as a grumble. He laid nose to bowl but didn't take his eyes off of her, and she turned away from him to watch the bag inside the microwave grow larger with every kernel that popped. "I don't get it, do you? Why here? Why again? It's weird, right?"

The microwave dinged and she found a bowl to empty the bag into, her mind on a certain man who now lived a matter of streets away. Why Carolina Cove?

She carried her gourmet dinner into the living room with her and curled up on the couch. Frankie found the remote, muting the volume and flipping through channels as she tried to distract herself from thoughts of Grayson.

It didn't work but she tried. Hard.

He'd looked good. A little tired and definitely frustrated at finding out his kid was probably a thief, but good. Handsome as ever with his dark hair and sexy, whisker-scruffed face.

No, not sexy. Deceitful, lying, secret-keeping…

Sexy face.

She closed her eyes and groaned, wondering if there would ever come a day when she could think of him and all that'd happened and not be sad.

A noise interrupted her thoughts and she stilled. What the heck was that?

It took her a few seconds to realize it was Tank's stomach growling. "Really?"

He didn't move other than to stare at her with those guilt-projecting eyes.

She waited, watched. Narrowed her gaze because she felt her resolve slipping. "You are unbelievable," she said, setting the popcorn on the coffee table beside her glass to stand.

She crossed to the kitchen and swiped a spoon from the drawer. "Shame on you."

She lowered herself to the floor with her back propped by the couch behind her, wineglass in hand because *she* was apparently more screwed up than her dog because *she* not only fell for unavailable men but she also catered to demanding dogs who ruled her with sad eyes and growling stomachs.

Tank lifted his head from his paws and bit down on his kibble bowl, carrying it with him to where she sat. "You are a *needy* hound, you know that? It's not attractive. How did you ever make it through basic?"

Tank set his bowl down on the floor by her hip before settling on his haunches to wait.

Frankie took a hefty sip of wine and played stare down with Tank, but they both knew who'd already won. Grumbling under her breath, she dipped the spoon into his kibble and lifted it for him to accept. "I'm the one who's upset here, you know. You should be feeding *me*."

Tank's large mouth opened and she dumped the spoonful inside. He chomped and swallowed and waited again.

Frankie glared at him, took another sip of wine, and filled the spoon. "It's a good thing you're cute. Otherwise you'd be sleeping on the couch tonight."

Chapter 5

Grayson sat outside on the entry porch of the house and stared down at his laptop. He hadn't allowed himself to search for Frankie since he'd moved to town because he'd told himself he'd only do it if—like in the past—life brought them together again.

He'd learned a long time ago that life often surprised him, and as of tonight, he wasn't disappointed. Circumstances had literally brought Frankie to his doorstep, and this time he wasn't going to let this opportunity pass or screw it up again, no matter the tension between them.

He'd made a huge mistake by keeping his marital situation from Frankie and then trying to break it to her the way he had. He'd tried so hard to free himself, but Daria had made it impossible, especially from half a world away. It had been over between them for years, but Daria had made a game of avoiding the court papers asking for a divorce. And in the midst of war, his priorities had been on the soldiers in his care.

Gray typed in Frankie's name and location and hit enter. The screen immediately filled with articles about her family, but he wasn't interested in those. She had been honest with him, told him about her military father and how her family had come to settle in Carolina Cove. No, he wanted to see her because like a man in the desert who sees an oasis, the single glimpse of her earlier wasn't enough.

Once more the screen filled with images, faces of people with Frankie's name or some version of it. He quickly scanned them until he found her, smiling, beautiful, holding a large fish as part of a tournament at the pier. "You and those boots."

The photo revealed Frankie wearing combat boots despite the sun blazing overhead. Not the most attractive feminine footwear but, for her, perfect. He'd teased her about favoring them even in her off-duty time. She'd said they tended to do some men-weeding for her so she didn't have to bother.

"I'm back," Christopher said.

Grayson looked up and realized he'd been so engrossed in the images and memories that his son had nearly made it into the house without him noticing. *Not going to win best parent award doing that.* "Stop. We have to talk."

"I have homework."

"It can wait," he said, closing the laptop and carrying it with him as he stood. "We have to talk."

"I have stuff I need to do, remember? My room?"

"It can wait." Gray locked eyes with Christopher and motioned for the boy to enter the house ahead of him. "Kitchen. Now."

Christopher did his usual eye roll and groan of complaint but did as ordered. Grayson followed him and saw the moment Chris spotted the bike part on the countertop.

"What's that?"

Gray had to give it to the kid. If he'd stolen the part and sold it to Frankie's garage, he didn't reveal it. "Bike part I ordered."

Christopher didn't say anything else but went to the fridge to search out the pizza leftovers and find himself a drink. And since the kid was going to play dumb, Gray decided to wait him out. Accusing Christopher of stealing wasn't the way to get on his good side, and while he was fairly sure Chris was the guilty party, the part could have been stolen off of the porch. He'd been meaning to get one of those door cams but hadn't gotten around to it. Now it was a priority.

"You just gonna stare at me? I really do have a lot of homework."

"Then maybe you should've stayed home instead of going out with your girlfriend."

Chris shrugged. "She asked me to walk on the beach. She was sad and she's been there for me when I'm sad. I was just being a good friend."

As a physician's assistant now working in the public sector, Gray knew the statistics for teens and depression. Knew Christopher was at high risk for issues due to his mother's death. "I'm glad you have someone to talk to, but you know you can talk to me about anything, right?"

Chris made a sound and shoved half a piece of pizza into his mouth.

"Look, Chris, I know things have been weird between us because of me being deployed so much of your life. I get it, but I'm home now and I want that to change. Especially with your mom gone—"

"Don't," Christopher said around a mouthful. "She's not gone—she's dead."

"Chris—"

Christopher swiped another piece of pizza from the box atop the counter and bolted for the door. Ah, man. "Chris—"

"I have homework to do."

"Christopher, come on. Let's talk about this."

"Leave me alone!"

Christopher tore out of the kitchen with his pizza and drink in hand and ran up the stairs as fast as his long legs could carry him. Gray watched him go, torn between letting Christopher calm down and following him.

Gray walked over to the part and opened the box to stare down at it. Obviously it wasn't safe to keep things like this around the house without Christopher or the porch pirate potentially stealing them so—

He smiled, an idea forming as he left the box behind to return to his laptop. Finding Frankie's garage wasn't difficult. Especially when the owner was as beautiful and talented, not to mention pro-community and military. Business hours on Saturday, too.

He clicked back on images and stared into Frankie's angled face.

Step one for gaining her forgiveness formed in

his head, and he toasted her photo with his water bottle. "Here's to next time, Frankie."

FRANKIE WALKED into London's Lattes around one the following afternoon with one thing in mind —work. She liked to immerse herself in work, and fixing things channeled all of the pent-up energy and frustration boiling inside of her since spotting Grayson on the other side of his front door.

"Hey, Tank. How's my boy?"

Frankie let go of Tank's required-by-law leash, which signaled his release to go greet her twin. London slipped Tank a treat, and Tank carried the gift with him to the floor below Frankie's chosen seat at the bar. "You by yourself today?"

"For a bit. The gang will be in soon. Looks like you had a rough night."

"Couldn't sleep."

"What are you doing today or do I even need to ask? You know you *are* still on vacation and—"

Something must have shown in her expression, because London broke off with a gasp.

"What? *What's* happened? Something to do with what you told me yesterday? Well, *say* something."

Frankie pointed to the coffeepots. "Fuel first."

"You haven't had coffee yet?"

"Didn't fall sleep until really early this morning so no coffee or food. Where's the kid?"

"Who? Oh, Joey? He was here around nine but not to work. He paid me cash for the stuff and left."

London hastily poured a large glass mug full to the brim, no doubt so Frankie couldn't take her to-go cup and *go*. "He probably told his helicopter parent and they caved. Who knows?"

"Here," London said as she set a mug in front of Frankie. "You want a sandwich? Muffin?"

"No. Just this."

"Start talking."

"It's him."

"Well, I figured that much just by your expression, but how did you find out for sure?"

Frankie explained about Steve purchasing the bike part and how the slip had led her to Grayson's door.

"That is… That is beyond bizarre."

"Tell me about it."

"I mean, *why* does it keep happening? Are you *sure* he's not stalking you?"

"Yes, Londy. It's just… What am I going to do? He lives here now. Works here."

"And you truly believe it's all a coincidence?"

"It's happened so many times before, so yes. I do."

"Okay, so you show up, part in hand to return, see that it's him, and then what?"

The door opened again with a jingle of the bell above it, and Frankie automatically bent to secure Tank's leash, because when people saw him, mothers of children especially, they tended to give the large shepherd a wide berth.

Frankie waited while London filled the family's order and cashed it out, sipping her brew while petting Tank, who seemed to be giving the wall connected to the counter his attention.

Frankie leaned sideways on the stool, but her view beyond the wall was of an empty chair and part of the table. Her guess was that, farther down the area, one of the patrons had a snack-size dog tucked on a lap or something.

"Okay, I'm back," London said. "Now tell me everything. Don't leave out a single detail."

Frankie inhaled at the demand and tried hard not to remember how Grayson's handsomeness had nearly floored her upon sight. "Well, he said his son can't seem to stay out of trouble, so I'm guessing he's the kid who sold to the part to Steve, but that hasn't been confirmed. Gray asked me to come inside to talk, but I said no. He grabbed my arm—didn't hurt me," she rushed to clarify when London's expression changed to one of fiery protection, "and Tank rushed to the rescue."

"Good boy, Tank," London said to the dog. "I hope you got a good taste."

Tank turned his head from the direction he still stared to glance at London, but just as quickly went back to whatever it was that held his attention.

"Yeah, Gray was afraid of losing a hand, so he let go and… I left. End of story. Oh, and he said his wife is dead."

London leaned her elbows against the counter and stared at Frankie.

"Wow."

"I know."

"No, I mean, how can you drop a bomb like that and say that's it? End of story? Aren't you curious? Didn't you ask what happened?"

"No. I don't care because what does it change?"

"Maybe it doesn't change anything but there's obviously a story there. Maybe she was sick? Like, terminally sick? Not that that's an excuse for lying to you."

"Exactly. It's not. So what could he possibly say

to make any of that okay?" She shook her head and took a long pull from the cooling coffee. "No, I think it's best if I don't know. It's… Londy, I really, really liked him and it was all a lie."

"I know. I'm sorry. But I wonder…"

"What?"

"I just wonder about the details. Nothing is ever black and white, and I get the feeling you're not telling me everything about his reaction to finding you on his doorstep."

"There's nothing left to tell."

"You're scared," London stated abruptly. "Oh, hon, I see it. And you have hard-core legitimate reasons to be. I get it. Obviously you aren't meant to be together despite the number of times he's appeared in your life. But I know you and you don't fall for anyone that easily, so there was something tangible there. Something worthy. Maybe talking to him and learning the actual details could help you? Give you some closure so you can move on?"

"I'm not sure I want to know, though. How do you believe someone after they've lied to you?"

"True."

Frankie downed the lukewarm coffee and stood. "I have to get to work."

"But—"

"I can't think straight right now, Londy. I'm too weirded out by the fact he's here."

GRAYSON WAITED until Frankie and Tank left the coffee shop and he heard the sound of her powerful Jeep drive away before he stood from the table he occupied in London's Lattes. He'd stopped into the coffee shop a half hour or so before Frankie's arrival to get some lunch and gather his thoughts before going to her garage.

He left the table and went back to the counter, waiting patiently for London—Frankie's twin—to look up from her task.

"Can I help you? Oh, hi, again," she said, having waited on him earlier. "Can I get you something else?"

"Two large coffees, both black, to go. And a half dozen of those chocolate oatmeal cookies."

"Someone's getting a nice surprise," London said, pouring the coffees and arranging them on a carryout tray before getting cookies from the display case.

He smiled, knowing they were Frankie's favorite. "I hope so."

London rang up the purchase and gave him the

total, but instead of using cash as he had earlier, he pulled his debit card from his wallet and handed it to her.

She swiped his card without looking.

"Thank you, Mr.— " She gasped sharply, her gaze moving from the slip to his face. "*You're*…?"

"Grayson Carter," he said, dipping his head. "It's nice to finally meet Frankie's twin. Thank you for what you said earlier. The details are important."

London's beautiful face flooded with hot color, and Grayson waited for her to come at him with a feminine barrage of sibling protectiveness.

"Well, we can add eavesdropping to your flaws."

"Sorry. But when the conversation is about me, I tend to listen. I don't intend to hurt Frankie."

"You already have—are—just by being here."

He picked up the coffee and the cookies. "I'm not a stalker. The company I hired into is based out of Virginia Beach."

"But you're here."

He smiled and nodded. "I was just as surprised as you look right now when they asked me to relocate."

"Because you *knew* she was here."

He gave her a short nod. "I knew she planned to

return home once she was out of the military, but I didn't know anything beyond that when I moved. I... hoped, though."

London shoved her hair away from her face and stared at him with open-mouthed bemusement.

"Hoped," she repeated. "That's a bold sentiment coming from a man already married to someone else."

"It's—"

"Complicated. Yeah, she told me."

"She couldn't have told you everything, because she wouldn't listen to me long enough to hear it for herself. But I ask that you give me a chance to make things right before you judge." A smile pulled at London's lips and Grayson frowned. "Something funny?"

"No. Not at all. But you don't expect Frankie to accept an apology after you lied to her, do you? You broke her trust and she doesn't take that lightly. None of us do."

"No one should." He lifted the coffee and cookies in his hands and nodded. "But I plan to make up for it somehow. I'll let you know how it goes," he said, holding Frankie's favorites in his hands. He turned to leave but paused, nodding to one of the items on display. "That friend of hers have any favorites?"

London followed his gaze to see what he referred to and gave him a narrow-eyed glare.

"Come on. I just want to talk to her."

Frankie's twin muttered to herself but retrieved a bag and filled it with several dog treats.

Gray emptied his hands and pulled out his wallet. "Thanks."

London cashed out the payment.

"You seem to be working awfully hard at this."

He gathered up his purchases again. "She's worth the effort."

"That she is. Wish I could believe the same about you."

MINUTES LATER GRAYSON pulled to a stop in the parking lot of the garage and took a deep breath before he cut the engine. He gathered the coffee and bags and left the vehicle, more nervous than a teenager on his first date.

"Sorry, we just closed. You can make an appointment for next week though," a man said. The name sewn into his shirt read Toby.

"Thanks, but I'm here for her," he said, spying a

familiar sight of tan legs and combat boots sticking out from under a Camaro.

Grayson was aware of the man's narrow-eyed perusal as he made his way into the bay. He'd no sooner walked up to where she lay on a mechanic's creeper than Frankie's grease-covered hand emerged and felt around on the concrete for a tool two inches from her reach. He used his foot to nudge it closer, and in the process, her hand landed briefly atop his shoe.

"Thanks."

"No problem."

Her lower torso and legs tensed. A second passed. Two.

"Yo, Frankie, you have a visitor," Toby called from one of the other bays. "And I'm outta here. Gonna shut it all down but the one you're in."

"Yeah. Thanks, Tobe," she called from under the car.

"I'll open the office door, too," the man said.

Frankie didn't respond and the bay doors lowered under Toby's direction. Grayson stood there, coffee and bags in hand, wondering why the office door needed to be open. He quickly found out when Tank appeared and planted himself beside Frankie's legs while giving Grayson the evil eye. "You, uh, going to come out from under there any time soon?"

"No. Don't think so."

"Do you think I won't climb under there with you? Wouldn't be the first time." Once, in Kabul, he'd gone to see her and found her working on a decades-old Army Jeep in her downtime. Rock music played, her boots had tapped to the beat, and he'd spent two hours in 110-degree heat beneath the vehicle helping her go over every inch of it. Just to spend time with her.

Now, though, he wondered if attempting such a move would get him a nice-sized dog bite. He carefully set the coffee tray and cookies atop the roof of the car and opened the second bag, keeping a sharp eye on Tank. The dog's nose twitched and he lifted his head to get a better whiff. Without a word, Gray broke the favored treat in half and slowly flattened his left palm toward the dog, willing Tank to take the offering.

The dog's gaze flicked back and forth between the treat Gray held and the bag in his other hand, and Grayson bit back a low chuckle. He dipped into the bag and gathered all but one of the treats, silently offering them to the dog.

The temptation apparently proved to be too

much for the gray-muzzled shepherd, because he rose and hopped over Frankie's legs to approach Grayson. Gray held still, maintained eye contact with the dog, and felt the dog's large canines scrape lightly against his skin as he gathered up the treats. Slowly, oh so slowly, Grayson turned his hand over for the dog to get an even better sniff. After a second or two of that, Grayson braved a light, quick rub of the dog's head and ears as Tank pulled away and retreated to drop the goodies on the ground by Frankie's legs but didn't eat them. The dog had patience, Grayson had to give him that.

The grit beneath the wheels of the creeper raked like broken glass against Grayson's nerves as Frankie slowly rolled from beneath the vehicle. The moment he locked gazes with her, he felt himself get sucked into the beautiful blue depths.

"Bribing my dog?"

"Just making friends."

"What are you doing here?"

He removed the tray and second bag from atop the roof and held up his peace offerings. "You didn't get your second cup."

A muffled word emerged from her full lips and color filled her face. After a moment, he squatted down, holding out the tray for her to take one of the cups. "Your sister is right, you know. It's not black and white."

"You… You should've freaking said something. Let us know you were there."

"I was too fascinated by the conversation."

"That's cheating… but I guess you're used to it."

He took the blow in stride because, if he was honest, he'd had feelings for a woman other than his wife from the moment he'd laid eyes on Frankie, but he'd never crossed the line. "I'd asked for a divorce before I ran into you that second time in California. Daria avoided the officials so she couldn't be served, even though she'd been cheating on me throughout our entire marriage, such as it was."

Frankie blinked at him, her ocean-blue eyes narrowing so much he saw her battle walls go up. Her gaze dropped to the tray and he lifted it again, motioning for her to take one.

"Why should I believe you?"

Her mouth curled down at the corners, but she lifted her grubby hands to pull a cup from the tray and took a fortifying sip. Oh, yeah. He remembered her coffee addiction and took full advantage. "Because it's true. And it's trackable if you trace the dates on the documents and the deputies' comments about not being able to find her. She fought me at every turn, cost me a small fortune, and moved around constantly so she couldn't be served. She made life impossible from half a world away."

Frankie broke eye contact and planted her boots on the concrete, getting to her feet with a painful-looking grimace. "What's wrong? Are you hurt?"

A low laugh emerged from her and she backed away from the hand he'd stretched out in order to help her.

"Thanks for the coffee. Leave the cookies and get out."

Chapter 6

Frankie set the coffee aside on her way to the ladies' room and locked the door behind her before giving into a full-blown, can't-breathe, how-is-this-possible panic attack. She turned the water on full blast and shoved her hands under the cold, watching the grime from her hands dirty the sink but not come off.

Why him? Why now?

Why hadn't she stuck around long enough in Kabul to hear his story and—

What? Be the other woman?

Because the fact of the matter was, at that time, he was still married. No ifs, ands, or buts. And she respected herself enough to never cross that line.

Marriage might only be a piece of paper to some, but to her it was more. So much more.

Integrity. Morals. Married was married. Period.

But now? He wasn't.

Did it matter, though?

She groaned aloud and winced at the sound it made echoing back at her from the tile wall and mirror. She spied the girly-smelling soap that would do little to clean her hands and regretted that she hadn't grabbed the heavy-duty cleanser off the shelf on her way in. And the coffee and cookies. She hadn't looked inside the bag but she knew what was in there. Oatmeal chocolate chip, her favorite.

One of her late-night debates with Grayson had centered around the best cookie ever eaten. She'd won by breaking out her mama's care package, which had contained said cookies from a local bakery, the same one London used for her baked goods at the coffee shop.

Frankie washed her hands as best she could and wondered if Grayson would give up and leave or if he waited outside for round two. She inhaled and wished she could think straight. Maybe then she'd know how to proceed.

She gripped the edges of the sink and closed her burning eyes. Yeah, sleep would help her think more clearly, but that wasn't going to happen. She had to go out there, see if he was still there, and figure out the next step after that.

Frankie opened her eyes and met her gaze in the mirror. "It's a test," she whispered. "Or an opportunity. The trick is to figure out which one."

A noise on the other side of the door drew her attention and she turned off the water, listening.

"So what do you think? Will she forgive me?" Grayson asked.

Frankie frowned, wondering who he was talking to and how she'd never before noticed the lack of soundproofing in the bathroom because of the door. Usually the guys had music playing in the bays and the television was typically on in the waiting area but still—

"I didn't mean to hurt her. I care about her. Have from the beginning. It's what made all of this so complicated."

Frankie blinked, remembering how he'd said that before, that night when things had gone so wrong. Complicated was such a lousy description for something so much bigger.

"So here's the deal," Grayson said. "You and me, we have to become buds, right? Because I know if you're not on my side, I don't stand a chance. So what do you say, Tank? Huh? Will you help me get the girl?"

Frankie twisted the knob and opened the door, her gaze locking on Grayson where he sat on the garage floor facing the ladies' room. Tank glanced back at her from where he stood at eye level with Grayson, and she knew Grayson had made himself vulnerable to the powerful and well-trained dog on purpose.

"There she is. Come on, buddy. What do you say, Tank? You got my six on this? Help me convince her to listen and hear me out?"

Tank turned his attention back to Grayson, and the moment Grayson held out his hand and Tank gave Grayson his paw in exchange for a treat, Frankie sighed. Men. Her four-legged hero had just turned traitor.

Grayson shook with Tank and gave the dog the treat before slowly standing.

"You may have swayed my dog with treats, but coffee and cookies won't do it for me."

Grayson grinned. "I'd be disappointed if it did. So how about I start with the truth, all of it, and we go from there?"

GRAYSON HELD his breath as he waited on Frankie's response. He could tell she was on the fence about whether or not to kick him out or hear him out, so the next few seconds ticked by with excruciating slowness.

"You're not going to give up, are you?"

"No," he stated, a firm shake of his head confirming his words. He'd waited so long, hoping for another chance with her, and now that it had happened, now that she'd literally appeared on his doorstep, he wasn't about to give up.

"Fine. Start talking."

"No. We do this right. You—and Tank, if he makes you feel safe—come with me."

She blinked up at him, her blue eyes wary.

"I have work to do. I've been gone for over a week and—"

"Frankie… the conversation we need to have requires more than five minutes in a garage with you sidestepping me every time I get close." He was pretty sure he heard her mutter *so stop stepping close* under her breath. "Come with me. Please."

She paced across the room and grabbed some hand scrub before moving to a utility sink across the way.

"Fine."

It wasn't the most agreeable tone but he'd take what he could get. "Tell me how to help you lock up."

She washed the grime from her hands, and then they spent the next couple of minutes making sure the garage was secure before heading toward his truck.

Frankie was quiet and he could tell she was overthinking.

"I should drive."

"I'm driving." She stopped where she stood, and he could practically hear her boot heels digging into the asphalt beneath them.

"Tank can't make that jump into your backseat. He'll screw up the pins in his legs if he tries it."

Pins? He looked at the elderly dog and wondered what all he'd survived. "Hey, buddy. Come here." Grayson unlocked the truck and opened the rear seat door. "No biting me, got it?"

He bent and very carefully wrapped his arms around the dog's body to lift him into the truck, all too aware of Tank's snout and those teeth having full access to his neck, arm, and shoulder in the process. "In you go. Good boy."

Grayson stepped back and shut the door once the dog was inside. Next, he opened the passenger door for Frankie and waited. She wanted to bolt, but he now had her dog and there was no turning back.

"Where are we going?"

"You'll see."

She glared at him for a long moment before giving in with a roll of her eyes and a huff.

Seconds later he was behind the wheel and the three of them were on their way toward the sound end of the island. Frankie alternated between staring out the window and glancing at him when she thought he wasn't aware of it.

He slowed his speed due to the traffic turning to take the ferry and thanked God for the timing when he spotted the short line of vehicles moving rapidly. He quickly turned and ignored her sharp gasp.

"We're going to Southport?"

"You need to eat something and the ride will give us a chance to talk."

"You just bought me cookies, and we could *talk* in Carolina Cove."

"Relax. It's a beautiful day for a ferry ride. Right, Tank?" He glanced at Frankie as he rolled to a stop to hand cash to the woman in the booth.

"You're all set. Perfect timing."

"Thanks," he said to the woman. To Frankie he

added, "Amazing how that keeps happening, isn't it? Kind of like the universe knows something we don't?"

She didn't comment. Not that he really expected her to.

Tank stared out the window from the back, pink tongue hanging as he watched the goings-on with interest.

Grayson drove onto the ferry as instructed and cut the engine after rolling down the windows. The majority of riders chose to go up top for a better view, but sitting as high as they did in the truck and with Tank to consider, Grayson simply unbuckled his seat belt and shifted to get more comfortable, wishing there was a way to fast-forward so that the story was out and they had already moved on to whatever happened next. "I joined the Marines when I was eighteen. The military was my way to college. I was six years in and still as stupid as ever when I found out my dad had cancer. I'd just re-upped at that point, which was good since he needed help covering expenses."

Grayson glanced at Frankie and found her staring out the windshield, her gaze locked on some distant point. "As soon as I was able, I came home. By then he was pretty bad off. The chemo and radiation... Daria... She was the wild girl next door. The kind of girl mamas warn their sons about. But when I got to the house that day, she was cleaning up my dad after he'd been sick like it was perfectly normal. In her house, the mess came from partying too hard, but again, not unusual to her. She'd hidden her pregnancy as long as she could, but her father had found out a few weeks before and kicked her out. My dad found her sleeping in his backyard shed and let her stay in my old room. She was grateful. So was I."

He inhaled and tried to find that spot that seemed to bring Frankie peace. "We kept in touch after I reported back. Daria updated me about my dad, and I asked about the baby. Every chance I got to go see my dad, I did. She was still there caring for him, getting bigger every day, and more and more scared about the future. Getting married seemed to make sense at the time. I had the stability she needed; she took excellent care of my dad. It was... an arrangement at first, but we agreed if we did it, it would be real and we'd make a go of married life. It worked for a while. Mostly because she had my dad watching her and Christopher to care for. Once my dad passed on, though... she started partying like she had in the old days, sleeping around. I'd go home and buddies would… avoid me. And I was naive enough to not understand why for way too long. I didn't want to face it.

"By the time I got my head on right, it was too late. At least I thought it was. I was deployed, going to school. A dad to Chris when I could be. You know how the military works. How hard it is on the family left behind. I thought maybe if I held on, things would work themselves out, and I wouldn't have to give up Chris."

Memories flooded his mind with every word. Grayson watched a bird dip and soar in the distance and knew those highs and lows. Knew the crazy that came with mistakes and heartbreak and the realization that he'd royally screwed up. "I could've been a better husband," he said simply. "I was never home, and we were strangers going into it. It was doomed from the start, but I thought I was doing the right thing at the time. I thought it could work. We could work."

"How did she die?"

It was the first time Frankie had spoken in a while, and her voice emerged husky and soft, like she'd been drawn into the emotion of the story as much as he had the memories of the good times, few though there were. "Car accident. She made it to the hospital but… I had to decide to keep her on machines or let her go. She had no brain function, complete organ failure. Too much damage. Chris blames me."

"I'm sorry."

"Me, too. For Christopher's sake. It sounds cold and I don't mean for it to, but our relationship was over the first time she cheated. I was done. I knew in Kabul when we almost… I knew that if I ever got another chance to see you and explain, I *had* to be free no matter what it took. I'd tried before but let things lapse when the papers couldn't be served.

"I didn't let anyone know I was coming back. I caught her at the house and she couldn't avoid it. Me. She begged me not to leave her. We argued and she… she even tried to seduce me. Like that would somehow fix what was wrong with us. I made her sign the papers by threatening to track down every one of her affairs to have her considered unfit. It was low. She was basically a good mother, but I was desperate. So she signed."

He heard Frankie inhale and turned to find her staring at him, her expression a mixture of horror and sorrow and shock.

"Why do I get the feeling that's not the end of it?"

"Because it wasn't," he said. "After she left, I slept... and I mean *slept*. I rested in a way I hadn't been able to in years. I woke up to strange noises, though. Crashes and... She was in the garage taking a baseball bat to the Harley my dad had given me. She'd been drinking. I grabbed the bat when she took a swing at me and her blouse pulled up and I knew... why she was so desperate. She was pregnant."

"Oh, wow."

"Yeah. By another loser who'd left as soon as she told him." He ran a hand over his head, pinched the back of his neck. "She got away from me. Got in her car and locked the doors and took off before I could stop her. She wrecked a few miles later. And now I'm father to a kid I don't know, who hates me and blames me for his mother's death, and... I'm here."

Silence followed his words, and he stared out the windshield, letting the quiet settle over them.

"Craaaaap."

He blinked at the statement and turned to look at her.

"I really didn't want to forgive you."

He fought off the smile that tried to form. "But?"

"I… get it. I don't know why you were so stupid for so long, but I get how complicated it was to divorce. It's bad enough doing that with both parties in the same city, much less a world away."

He leaned toward her only to stop when she immediately held up a palm to stop him.

"I said I forgive you, Grayson. But that doesn't change the fact you lied to me."

Chapter 7

Frankie stared out the window at the passing scenery as Grayson drove from the ferry dock toward Southport's waterfront. They'd remained in silence ever since she'd said it didn't change things because… it didn't. The ferry had approached the shore and the announcement sounded for passengers to return to their vehicles. With the windows down and the cars so closely parked, discussing anything without an audience was impossible. Not that there was much left to be said.

She wished she could hear Grayson's thoughts. Did he really think it would be that easy? He was sorry, it was bad, forgive me, let's… what? His story explained a lot of things, but facts were facts. He could have told her. Should have. Long before Kabul.

"Do you have any favorite places to eat?"

Eat? She'd thought he'd turn the truck around and get right back on the ferry to take them home, but he'd driven off the ramp and down the road. Now he wanted to eat?

"You forgive me. It's a start. So let's have some food."

"And then?" she asked. "You lied to me about something *big*. Majorly big. Trust is—"

"Everything. And I screwed up. It wasn't that I didn't plan on telling you, it was a matter of when. I wanted to be free. I wanted it to be part of my past."

"But if you care for someone, you don't keep secrets. You share things—especially big things."

"I know. I realize that now. I should have realized it then, but I didn't, and I will *always* regret that. Look, sweetheart, I'll do whatever it takes to get you to trust me again. Just give me a chance. Can you do that?"

Her stomach chose that moment to growl, and she hoped the music playing in the background and the air blowing from the vents disguised it. But a glance at his face and the handsome grin he wore said he'd heard it loud and clear. "I skipped break-fast and we didn't bring the cookies."

"So what are you in the mood for?"

Did she want to sit through a meal with him? Want to stare across the table from him like couples did, even though they weren't and never would be?

This may be your only chance.

Truth be told, just once she'd like the experi-ence. To be out with Grayson like a normal couple on a normal date. Before having to say goodbye because she was a hypocrite and *couldn't* share the big thing now in her life that was so devastating. "I… know a good hot dog and burger place. It's down by the waterfront."

The next mile and a half didn't take long, and minutes after parking, Grayson went inside the restaurant to place their order while she and Tank walked toward the water. Southport was busy with end-of-season travelers, but she spotted an older couple leaving a swing and picked up her pace to snag the prime spot.

Tank settled in on the ground in the shade behind the swing, and she wished she'd thought to ask Grayson to get a bottle of water for Tank. Now she'd have to wait until Grayson appeared to go get one.

Her phone went off and she glanced at the text.

Where are you? I dropped by the garage and you didn't answer. You okay?

London never came to the garage. And seeing as how the coffee and cookies had come from London's Lattes, she wondered how much her sister knew. *Not working today,* she texted.

Well, obviously. Are you okay? I'm worried about you.

Tank's favorite dog treats were a bit much, don't you think?

Silence. The three little dots indicating London typed came and went multiple times but a message didn't appear. Finally the dots appeared again and then—

I'll leave you be but call me ASAP! I mean it!

Frankie inhaled and sighed, wondering how twenty-four hours could change so much.

"Nice spot."

She looked up to find Grayson approaching with their food and drinks—and a bottle of water and empty cup for Tank. He was a considerate liar if nothing else, she mused. Oh, she knew she was being harsh, because people made mistakes. She'd made plenty herself and would make so many more before her life was over, but lying about a wife was a pretty big one, right?

"Thanks," she said, reaching for her bag to grab some cash.

"If you're doing what I think you're doing, stop."

"This isn't a date. You're not paying for my lunch."

"It's a hot dog—and I still owe you for the money you paid the kid for the taillight cover."

The kid? "So you don't think it was your son?"

Grayson settled onto the swing beside her and began pulling their hot dogs and onion rings from the bag. "It probably was given the way he's acted out since Daria's death but... I don't know, something kept me from accusing him."

"A kid was in London's two days ago. I caught him stealing birthday presents for his girlfriend."

"Did he have a name?"

"He said Joey, but I got the feeling it was a fake."

"Chris's girlfriend has a birthday party today. That's where he's at now."

She stared at Grayson, wondering if it was possible they *weren't* talking about the same kid. That was a pretty big coincidence but look at the two of them. Things happened.

Grayson met her gaze and apparently came to the same conclusion.

"Joey, huh?"

"London offered to let him work off the cost of the items but she said when he came in the next day, he paid her cash, took the stuff, and left."

"Let me guess—this took place after your guy paid cash for the part?"

She winced and shrugged.

"That would be a pretty big coincidence."

"Who knows? But she can't be the only teenage girl on the island having a birthday today, so maybe it is."

Grayson stared out at the sun sparkling off of the Atlantic, the hot dog seemingly forgotten in his large hands.

"What did the kid look like? Joey."

She described him and watched as Grayson's expression became even more grim. "I'm not helping, am I?"

"It's not your fault. I'd like to see one of the pictures London took of the kid, though."

Frankie texted London with the query along with a *don't ask* and London quickly texted back and Joey's face filled her screen. "There. That's him."

Grayson took the phone and forwarded the picture to a number she didn't recognize but guessed to be his. *Which means he now has yours. Oh, is this a good idea?* "That's him, huh?"

"Yeah."

She could see the pain the news caused Grayson. "I'm sorry."

"Me, too. He's… Christopher's had a hard time. His entire life, I was gone more than I was home, and now he's… a stranger. *I'm* a stranger. We butt heads at every turn. I didn't know he'd resorted to stealing, though."

"Hey, there's still a chance that he didn't get the money from the part. That could've been a different kid."

"Maybe. Chris said he'd found a stash of birthday money he'd forgotten about. But you caught Chris trying to steal the stuff first."

"Yeah, but he didn't seem like a pro to me. He was too nervous. Too obvious about it. Maybe he had a momentary lack of judgment and, when he found the money, went to London's to make good."

"Maybe."

"I… could pull my security footage," she offered. "See if the cameras got a shot of the kid. I had the system installed after one of my mechanics ripped me off. It's so new I forget it's there sometimes, but the feed records on the system at my house."

"That'd be great. We can look when we get back."

We? She'd meant that she would look but — "Uh…"

Grayson uncovered his wrapped hot dog and took a bite, and she did the same, finally getting around to feeding her noisy stomach.

"Man, these are good. That sauce is amazing."

She nodded and smiled, wondering how something as simple as a hot dog on the swing beside Grayson could feel so—

"Hey, Tank. Sorry, buddy. Here."

She turned her gaze away from the water to find Grayson opening the water bottle she'd forgotten about. He poured Tank a half a cup that the dog eagerly lapped up. "Thank you."

"No problem. He's a good—"

Boom!

Frankie scrambled off the swing toward the trees behind them, hunkering down as she searched for insurgents. Her heart pounded, racing in her chest when a *boom* sounded again, though not as loud.

"Frankie?"

She huddled on the ground, back against the base of a large tree. Tank approached and she grabbed the dog and pulled him across her lap, trying to make them both as small as possible to avoid getting hit by the—

Grayson.

People.

A few of them stared at her.

Whispered.

Dizziness engulfed her, and she leaned her head forward against Tank's panting body, feeling him shake almost as strongly as she did.

"Frankie?"

Tears flooded her eyes and burned but she refused to let them fall. She squeezed them tight, rubbed the excess moisture away on Tank's fur.

She swallowed hard and finally lifted her head, although she couldn't meet Grayson's gaze. He was a physician's assistant. Ex-military. No doubt he knew what he'd just witnessed.

Grayson approached her and Tank growled and bared teeth.

"Hey, buddy. Hey, it's okay. Just me."

He squatted down so that he was at eye level with her, but other than a quick glance, Frankie couldn't hold his gaze. He'd seen her mad scramble for shelter. And while she'd responded to a few things in the past, she'd somehow avoided reacting around family or friends, mostly by steering clear of anything that included fireworks or live ammo or noises that made her think *bomb*.

"Frankie, talk to me."

Tank's growl grew stronger and Frankie's entire body shook with the adrenaline rush now fading to shock.

"Frankie," Grayson said, his tone sharper than before. "Control your animal, soldier."

People were moving closer, and Tank was eyeing them all, growling because he reacted to her fear. If someone got hurt because of her...

She shifted her trembling hand from Tank's shoulder to his neck, not stopping until she turned the dog's muzzle toward her. She met Tank's gaze. "*Nein*," she said softly, her voice quaking. "*Nein, ruhig*," using German to tell Tank no and quiet. "*Vol-no*." *Relax*, she repeated to herself. "*Vol-no*. Good boy."

Tank immediately stopped growling at her words, but he trembled as badly as she did due to what had just happened. She began soothing the dog in a sad attempt to soothe herself. Would there ever be a day when a loud bang wouldn't be so terrifying?

A few seconds passed as she petted the dog, focusing on her breathing to try to bring it under control. She vaguely heard Grayson speaking softly to an older gentleman who approached him to ask if he could help, and wanted the ground to open up and swallow her. The man walked away and she had Grayson's full attention again.

"Frankie?"

"I'm good." She couldn't meet his gaze. Didn't want to see what she knew she'd see. "I-I'm good."

"I know. You want to go home?"

She nodded. Home. She wanted her dark bedroom and the weighted blanket recommended by her docs. Tank's big body in bed beside her. Thankfully she didn't have this type of reaction often, but when she did, it left her so depleted and exhausted she actually was able to sleep. Until the dreams kicked in and the cycle of stress and sleeplessness began again.

Grayson straightened, and after a moment, she pushed herself up the tree, uncaring that the bark scraped her back. Tank didn't growl but pressed his body against her calf, maintaining protective contact. She leaned heavily against the tree trunk until the ground stopped spinning.

"Can you walk?"

"Yes."

She could walk. She just couldn't stop shaking. It was humiliating. One step made her feel like a baby animal taking its first steps. "What— What was the n-noise?"

"Doesn't matter."

"What was it?"

Grayson inhaled.

"Construction up the street. A truck dumping its load by lifting and dropping the bed."

For the love of... Seriously? She'd made a complete fool of herself over a *dump truck?*

"Come on. Let's go." He held out his hand.

She took a step on her wobbly legs and prayed they held her up. They hadn't parked far away, but every step was an effort in concentration to keep her knees from buckling. Grayson's grasp on her elbow was firm, supporting.

Finally they got to his large truck and he opened the back door.

"Frankie, I don't want a dog bite here. Help me out."

She blinked, only then realizing Tank had his hackles up.

"Tank, *fuss*," she said so he would heel. "Friendly."

Grayson slowly bent and gently petted Tank for a few seconds before he cradled the shaking dog in his arms to lift him into the truck. Frankie stood there watching, weaving on her feet because she felt disconnected from her body.

When Tank was safely inside, Grayson opened her door, but she took one step toward the step bar and stopped. She honestly didn't think she had the strength or ability to get in.

Grayson must have guessed at her thoughts, because he bussed a kiss over her head before sweeping her up into his arms and depositing her on the seat. He yanked the seat belt from the base and wrapped it over her front, clicking it into place at her hip.

She sucked in a sharp breath, her mind flying back in time, envisioning the blast and the pain and the blood where his hands were now. A shudder rolled over her, the deafening sound. The ringing in her ears.

"You're okay, sweetheart. You're home now. It's okay."

Home. Yeah, she'd come home, but now they both knew she'd left a big part of herself in that desert.

Chapter 8

Grayson blasted the air to cool Frankie's too-hot and trembling frame and let her have some silence to regroup after what had just happened.

He knew PTSD when he saw it. The question was what had she encountered to cause it and when? Maybe he should've done a little more digging when he'd searched online.

Frankie had mentioned Tank's injury and how she'd come by the dog, but now he wondered if her choosing the animal had more to do with her own PTSD issues than simply wanting to help the dog live out the rest of his life with honor as a four-legged soldier.

He drove the two miles back to the ferry line for

the return trip. Frankie had her eyes closed, face toward the window, but he knew she wasn't asleep. Once he'd paid the fare and took his place in the marked lane to board, he cleared his throat. "I talked the entire way over here. It's your turn now."

She didn't respond.

"Frankie, I'm not giving up. And while I hate whatever it was that left you dealing with reactions like that, you know I get it. So talk to me. What happened?"

Nothing.

His hands tightened over the wheel but he heard her take a breath. The sound shattered him because it was such a shaky, shuddering inhalation.

"Roadside bomb. A convoy ambush. It was… We were pinned down for quite a while."

"Casualties?"

"Four. Two bled out at the scene and two later."

He'd treated more battle wounds than he wanted to think about, so he had an idea of what she'd seen. "I'm sorry."

"It's all part of it. I knew that when I signed up."

Being willing to sacrifice for your country was one thing but having to do it another. PTSD wasn't something to be taken lightly, nor should she be dealing with it on her own. "Do you see a counselor? Are you part of a group?"

He glanced at her in time to catch the wince that momentarily marred her beautiful features.

"I did. At the hospital in Germany. Not here."

"Frankie—"

"What? I'm busy. You think it's easy to run a business and work the way I do?"

"I think you can make time for something that will help you. You need to talk about what happened."

"No one needs to know that about me here."

"Why not? It means you're human."

"It means I'm crazy... or at least that's what a lot of people think when a sudden noise makes me jump through the roof o-or hide behind a freaking tree. They'd stop seeing *me* and start wondering if they're in danger because I know how to use a gun."

Grayson reached across the expanse and took hold of her hand. "Do you think your family wouldn't understand? Your father?"

During one of their many chats overseas, she'd told him about her family and her colonel father, every word full of praise and admiration.

"He'd understand but he'd also blame himself. Feel responsible somehow. I don't want that."

She tried to protect them, at cost to herself. "I'm glad you told me."

"I didn't *tell* you," she muttered. "I made a fool of myself and you saw it."

She closed her eyes again and he let her retreat. For the time being. At the moment, he was content with holding her hand until the last of the adrenaline shakes faded, and he drove them onto the ferry.

The ferry got underway, and after a while, her breathing changed, deepened, and he could tell she'd fallen into an exhausted sleep. He didn't release his hold but was content to stare across the expanse of the truck. There were plenty of beautiful women in the world, but he'd never met one who fascinated him as much as Frankie. Smart, beautiful, funny. She cared for her fellow man and worked to make the world a better place. She was the whole package.

Once they approached the ferry landing, he pulled out his phone and used an app to order them food. Frankie needed to eat and sleep, and he was going to see that she got both.

The alert asking passengers to return to their cars woke Frankie from her doze and she blushed when she found him watching her.

"Well, that's humiliating," she said.

"You're exhausted. When was the last time you slept through the night?"

"I-I sleep. Just not much."

"Well, you'll be happy to know there was no snoring except for Tank's. He's just as drained as you after the shakes wore off."

Frankie glanced at the dog in the backseat before turning her attention to him.

"Wow. We're a fun party, aren't we?"

He laughed at her dry tone and lifted her hand to his lips. "We only got a bite of those hot dogs, so I ordered some dinner. I'll pick it up on the way to your place."

"I need to get my Jeep."

"It can wait. You're still shaky." He ignored her disgruntled glare and drove off the ferry to make the turn toward Carolina Cove.

"Shouldn't you... I don't know, go check on your son?"

Grayson didn't want to think of Christopher as a thief, but if he was... "Nothing I do right at this moment is going to change things if he is the one who sold that part to your guy. I'm furious enough about him trying to steal from your sister, so right now might not be the best time to confront him. It'll happen, though. Trust me."

Right now he needed to focus on the kick in the gut he'd had standing by so helplessly while watching Frankie melt down. It had torn him in two. He hated that she struggled but hated it more that she did so alone.

He stopped by the restaurant and picked up their order, and Frankie reluctantly gave him directions to her house after he refused a second time to drop her off at the garage. Her post-episode exhaustion presented itself in numerous ways, and even though she'd probably be fine behind the wheel, he didn't want to take any chances on her reflexes not being what they should.

He pulled up to her condo complex and parked in a visitor's spot. "Nice place."

"Yeah. I lucked into it as a temporary off-season rental when I got out of the military, and the couple have let me stay on full-time."

Grayson retrieved Tank from the back of the truck and fell into step beside Frankie as she walked to an elevator carrying the bag of food.

"Sixth floor," Frankie said when they were inside and he was closest to the buttons.

He snagged the bag from her hands, searching

her face. Frankie looked spent. Between the shadows beneath her eyes and the way her shoulders drooped, he wondered if he shouldn't pry into her medical history some more. See if she had medication to help her sleep? Something for anxiety?

Moments later they stood outside Frankie's door. Her fingers still shook slightly as she tried to put the key in the lock. "Let me."

He closed his hand over hers to steady her and heard her sharp inhalation because of how he stood behind her, cradling her from behind.

The door opened and she hurried inside.

The condo was older, dated in its colors and furnishings, but the view made up for it. The space had a small kitchenette with built-in island and stools for meals, a couch, chair, and television. There were no knickknacks or clutter, but there was a basket with a few dog toys near the wall by a small computer desk.

"Excuse me," she said, heading toward a door straight off the living room.

He spotted a sink and shower curtain inside. "Mind if I look around?"

"There's not much to look at, but sure."

She shut the bathroom door, and Grayson

turned to Tank. The dog watched him closely but seemed to accept the fact there was another male in the space. "Help me out here, buddy. How's she really doing?"

Tank cocked his head at the question, and Grayson frowned since it seemed like the dog had understood him. Tank headed toward the bathroom door but turned left. Grayson followed, curious as to where the dog went.

Tank hopped onto the bed and made himself comfortable.

Frankie's bedroom looked like any other. Bed, dresser, nightstand. It was the lack of clothing and other womanly items that revealed so much. Her closet door was open, and while it wasn't large by any means, her clothing still took up less than half the space. Frankie was not a materialistic woman or girly girl.

A glance down left him grinning, though. A sparkly set of four-inch heels sat beside a pair of combat boots. *That's my girl.*

Grayson turned away from the intriguing sight and paused to pet Tank. The dog sprawled atop a blanket, and something about it drew Grayson. He lifted the edge… weighted. The heavy beads inside shifted like noisy sand, but it went along with the episode he'd witnessed today. She wasn't in a group but she—or someone—knew the advantages of such a blanket. He studied the nightstand and spotted a medicine bottle tucked behind a lamp, almost out of sight. He wasn't someone who'd go through drawers or closets, but the items were in plain sight. And the bottle of sleeping pills looked to be full, despite the fill date. Ever the stubborn woman to not accept help where she could get it.

He carefully tucked the bottle back into place and moved down the short hall to the living room. The balcony doors opened with a press of the latch, and he stepped out to breathe deeply of the salt air and sunshine. He wasn't sure how much time Frankie spent out here, but he hoped it helped her as it did so many, and he was quickly discovering that fall at the beach was just as beautiful as summer.

Grayson heard the bathroom door open and turned to reenter the condo. Frankie had changed out of her sweat-dampened shirt into a tank top that revealed her tanned, toned arms. She'd also powdered her face in what was probably an attempt to hide the shadows under her eyes and added some mascara.

She was beautiful sans makeup, but the little

extra effort made her stunning. "Have I mentioned how amazing you look?"

"Thanks. I…" She plucked at the shirt. "I'm sorry again. About what happened."

"Stop apologizing. I'm glad I was there, though I'm well aware had I not kidnapped you, maybe it wouldn't have happened."

"It's okay. I'm good now."

He moved toward her slowly, not wanting to scare her off. When he was finally close enough to touch her, he lifted his hand to stroke his fingers over her silky cheek. "You want to tell me how often that happens?"

"Not very. I'm serious."

He accepted the statement at face value. "Good. You've got my number now. You can call or text anytime. I'll come over or listen. Whatever you need."

She held his gaze a long moment before looking away and wetting her lips.

"That's not necessary."

"Maybe not but it's an option, and it's yours."

"Thanks. But I mean it. It doesn't happen as much now. I think maybe it was the stress of traveling back from Florida and seeing y— uh, you know."

"I do. Seeing me hasn't been easy for you, but Frankie?" He waited until she met his gaze once more. "I meant what I said. I know I can't undo what I did, but I am sorry. I think a part of me knew you'd walk away if you knew the truth. I respect that about you. Your integrity is… tangible. That's one of the reasons I was trying to get free, because I didn't want to blow it. But here we are again, and that has to mean something, doesn't it?"

Her lashes lowered over her beautiful eyes, and he used the hand at her cheek to cradle her as he moved closer. Lowered his head until his lips hovered a breath from hers.

She smelled good. During her absence, she'd sprayed something on that made him think coconuts and fruity drinks. Maybe his combat girl was more of a girly girl after all.

Frankie trembled, though he knew it wasn't from fear or left over from her PTSD episode. The chemistry between them had always been strong, and this kiss… their first…

He savored the moment. Every inhalation, the way she looked at him, the feel of her hands gripping his arms, nails lightly digging into him. Finally he closed the distance and pressed his mouth to hers. He heard her gasp, captured her moan and the minty taste of her, pulled her closer and deep-ened the kiss until she broke away to gulp in a breath. She stared into his eyes a long moment before she tugged him low to kiss him again. And again.

All the wondering, the time apart, the waiting, was over. Every breath, every taste. She was as fabu-lous as he'd known she would be. "Beautiful. You are so beautiful."

The kissing continued, the contact and heat between them growing as each second passed, building to a level that had to be tempered. He wouldn't rush this. Not now. "Frankie, go out with me. Date me. Let's do this right," he murmured, kissing her neck, her jaw. Nipping the little lobe of her ear. "You can't kiss me like this, respond to me, and not want to know if more's—"

Frankie pushed at his shoulders, eyes wide as she stared up at him. She breathed as raggedly as he did, but while he was ready to do whatever it took to convince her to give him a chance, he could tell by her expression how she attempted to shore up the barriers again. "No. No, baby, don't back down from this. *Frankie*."

He took a step toward her, but she turned and bolted in the opposite direction.

"You *lied* to me."

"I'm sorry."

"Maybe you are. But what if it's just… curiosity? Kind of that forbidden love thing?"

"What?"

"What if"—she waved a hand in the air—"we feel this way because we keep running into each other like we have? What if it's just chemistry? Not real?"

"You know good and well that it's real, sweetheart. It's so real and powerful it scares you. It scares me, too, but I'm willing to see where it takes us because I have a feeling I already know."

He winced at the words and the impact they had on her. Quickest way to push a skittish woman too fast? Talk about the future. "Frankie… Frankie, stop retreating."

She'd backed up for each step he took toward her, stopping only when her back hit one of the stools at the island.

"I'm not."

He tried to read her expression but couldn't. "You kissed me back. If you're not as drawn to me and interested as I am, why did you do that?"

"Like I said, maybe it's just curiosity."

He crossed his arms over his chest and studied

her. "I'm not buying it. Tough girl Frankie is afraid. Why?" He watched her closely and could practically hear her mind cranking away, searching for every reasonable excuse.

"I'll… We should check the feeds. I'll log in and pull up the security footage."

"That can wait. I told you, Chris is at a party and accounted for. We need to settle this."

"Why? Why the sudden rush when we've waited this long?"

"I'm willing to wait as long as you need. I hurt you."

"Yes, you did. So how do I ever trust you again? *Why* would I trust you again? What you want from me is big, Grayson. You've lied to me once, you could do it again, and maybe I'm not willing to take that risk. Did you ever consider that?"

Grayson's arms tightened across his chest. She battled him at every turn and while he understood why, that it was his fault, it frustrated him to no end. No matter how badly he wanted to fast-forward into whatever came next between them, he had to go slow. Let her trust rebuild so she'd feel secure. "The food's getting cold. You need to eat."

She'd had a rough day and was dealing with far more than just him reappearing in her life.

"So that's it? You'll accept what I said and… we can just be friends?"

Friendship was a good base for the life he wanted with her, and it was time to call a truce. But no way was he conceding defeat when he wanted so much more. "Sure. For now."

Chapter 9

Spending the afternoon and evening with Grayson was not what she'd intended to do with her day. He'd ordered way too much food so there were plenty of leftovers, and after placing the containers in the fridge, he settled himself beside her on the couch and asked to watch a movie.

"You don't strike me as a movie buff."

"Ah, but I am. Pick one."

"You seem to be under the impression you're invited to stay."

"I thought we were friends? You'd kick me out?"

She frowned at his blatant advantage-taking and clicked on the television, deciding to see how long he'd last if she chose a rom-com.

She curled up in one corner of the couch while he took the other, and after a while it became really hard to keep her eyes open. Between her full belly, sleepless nights, and the most boring and unrealistic romance unfolding onscreen, she felt herself drifting.

Sometime later she sensed movement on the couch and forced her lashes high to see Grayson had scooted closer to her. He put his arm up along the back of the couch and gently tugged her toward him.

"You look really uncomfortable."

She leaned against his side, liking the way his body warmed hers. "I'm fine."

"Frankie. Come here."

She thought she felt his lips brush against the top of her head. "Don't get fresh," she mumbled, eyes closed.

"Wouldn't dream of it. Even if I know good and well the woman fighting me at every turn wants to be with me, too."

Oh, she did. The temptation was there. The interest. Could men and women be friends? She had guy friends. Most of them were interested in more, and she kept them at arm's length because she wasn't, but she could do the same with Grayson. *Not when you let him kiss you.* "She wants," Frankie said softly, "to not fight with you."

"Then don't," he whispered. "Forgive me and go out with me. A real date."

She pressed her face against his shirt, the hard chest beneath, and hated that he made her feel so…

Safe?

But how was that possible given what had happened between them?

She rolled her head along his shoulder to better see his face and stared up at him drowsily. "What if we're not meant to be more than friends and we ruin it by dating? And what about your son? You need to focus on him right now. Not… us."

Grayson smoothed his knuckles along her jawline and lowered his head, took her mouth in a kiss that stole her breath and curled her toes and made her head spin for all the right reasons. The kisses earlier weren't flukes, and as one kiss blended into more, she found herself pulled across his lap, cradled against him, lips meeting and parting in sweet, sultry kisses that lessened her fear and increased it at the same time.

"What if," he said against her mouth, "we're

meant to be so much more and we had to wait for the timing to be right?"

He kissed her again, lingering over the contact until she lifted her gaze and found him watching her. Their gazes locked and she couldn't look away, couldn't blink. Forgot to breathe.

"What if this could be everything we've always wanted? Everything we've dreamed of?"

What if. Oh, the what ifs were endless. Because what if he hurt her again? Not many men could handle someone with her issues, but a man like Grayson, a former soldier, someone in the medical field who understood what she dealt with… Could he? Would he?

Because what if the world imploded tomorrow? When life boiled down to its bits, all that mattered was who she loved and cared enough about to spend time with in those final moments. And given that no one knew the when or the how of a passing, any day could be the final one. Was she going to give up before she even got started? Grayson seemed remorseful. Sincere. What if… "Okay."

His gaze narrowed and he drew back a bit.

"Okay? We can… You're saying you'll date me?"

She smothered his words with her lips. His arm

tightened around her back and he groaned, pressing her closer and holding her in place while he kissed her over and over again.

After a long while, a noise intruded. She ignored it at first because she thought it was his phone, but when hers started ringing, the moment ended with a muttered complaint from Grayson and several quick, hard smooches that told her how much he didn't want to stop.

He let her slide off of his lap onto the couch beside him before removing his phone from his pocket.

"Hello?"

Frankie got up and moved to the island, where she'd left her cell upon their arrival. She picked it up and punched in the code to see a message from Carolina.

London said you might know this kid?

Oh, no. The picture was of Christopher. She winced and texted back as she crossed the floor to the computer. She needed to pull the security footage from her garage, and now might be a really good time to know the extent of Christopher's antics.

What did he do? she texted.

While she waited for Carolina's reply, Frankie

clicked on the day she'd arrived back in town and quickly moved through the footage an hour or so before she'd gone to the garage. The moment she saw a small-built shadow approach her mechanic, she stopped the footage to watch.

Oh, boy.

The photo quality was a little grainy but there was no doubt who the kid was.

A chime sounded.

Some kids tipped the claw machine and shattered it. They took off but Dad caught this one. I think Dad is on the phone with the kid's parents and the cops just walked in. Party at the pier house! :)

Frankie met Grayson's gaze and hurried over to where Grayson now paced. She waggled her fingers to ask for the phone, and when Grayson hesitated, she took it from his hands. "Dad, it's Frankie. Caro told me what's happening and… do your best to keep the police out of this, okay? We're on our way."

Her father sighed heavily in her ear.

"Where are you now?"

"My condo." As soon as the words left her mouth, she grimaced. "Grayson and I are… friends," she said, meeting Grayson's gaze. "Dad, just… go scary colonel dad all you want, okay, but see if you can keep the cops from charging Christopher. We'll figure the rest out once we get there."

"That's one way to make an impression with your father," Grayson muttered once she'd ended the call. "Thank you. For trying to keep the police out of it."

"Don't thank me yet. He may not be able to. Come on, let's go."

Grayson followed her toward the door but stopped in his tracks. She turned to find him staring at the image frozen on her computer screen. "Grayson? That can wait. One thing at a time."

WHAT IF IT *could be everything we've always wanted?*

The question ping-ponged in Frankie's head the entire way to the pier house.

What would happen when she told him the truth? If she revealed the full extent of her injuries, would that be it? For some men, the answer would be a definitive yes.

Carolina texted a couple more times asking who Grayson was since she'd overhead the conversation on their father's end, and Frankie silently groaned. Any hope of keeping her family out of her personal life was now gone, and once Carolina spread the word to the sisters.…

She really wasn't ready for this. Any of it.

They entered the pier house to find her father had pulled Christopher into the more private area in the middle of the building that served as storage, office, and jewelry display, and she grimaced when her first thought was that she hoped he'd locked the cases before allowing Christopher inside.

Grayson led the way, looking tall and imposing with his glower, and when Christopher spotted him, the boy's face paled.

"I didn't do it this time. I didn't," Christopher said, staring at Grayson with pleading eyes.

"Why should we believe you?" Grayson asked. "It's the third strike, Chris. And that's only the ones we know of."

"Third…?"

She stepped out from behind Grayson's broad form and Christopher's eyes widened.

"I know about the part you stole from me and pawned at Frankie's garage. What is *wrong* with you?"

Something inside of her forced her feet in motion. Frankie grabbed a plastic waste can and handed it to the kid just in time for him to get sick.

Oh, yeah. He'd definitely been drinking.

Grayson stared at his son and Frankie's heart broke at what she saw. She remembered his comment about them being strangers after Grayson served for so long, and she doubted any civilian knew the full price soldiers and their families paid during their enlistment.

Christopher stood as though to make a run for it, but her father put a hand on his shoulder and shoved the kid back down.

"Son, you sit in that chair until I tell you to get up. That's an order. Otherwise you *will* be talking to the police. You hear me?"

"Whatever."

"What was that?"

Christopher settled himself in the seat.

"I mean, yes, sir."

Her father straightened. "You two, over here."

Her father tilted his head toward the single entry/exit point, and she and Grayson moved to join him.

"Are you okay?" she whispered to Grayson, who seemed to be a combination of embarrassed and angry and struggling to find words to express it.

Grayson stared at his son, looking like a man very much in need of a stiff drink himself.

"Son, you aren't responsible for the stupid he's been doing, but you are responsible for your household. The boy and his friends shattered a claw machine with their antics, and it's a wonder someone wasn't seriously injured."

"I understand. I'm sorry, sir."

"Don't be sorry. I told the police you'd see that he was punished. I want to know how."

"How, sir?"

"How are you going to fix the mess that's sitting over there sobbing into his T-shirt when he's not vomiting and stinking up the place?"

"Boot camp," Frankie said softly, earning the attention of both men. "Whenever we got into trouble, we got boot camp. You always said we were better able to focus if we were too tired to act out and talk back. If he's running or exercising when he's not working to repay what he owes, he isn't stealing."

Grayson met her gaze and held it a long moment. "You think it'll work?"

"It did with us."

"Does that mean you'll help me with this? It might help with your—"

"Stress," she said before Grayson could tell her father about the PTSD. "Sure. I'll help."

Her father's thick eyebrows had lifted high at Grayson's question, but she ignored the too-keen awareness she found there after she'd cut Grayson off.

Like it or not, Grayson was right. The time spent exhausting herself might help her sleep so… why not?

"I have to agree, it worked with my girls," her father said. "Though, I should probably confess it was also a way for me to spend quality time with them. What?" her father said with a small smile at her. "The older I got, the harder it was to keep up. It was a win-win. And since you're helping, I'll pitch in, too. I can improvise some things under the pier house on the beach," her father said. "It's old-school but effective."

Grayson looked shocked by her father's offer, but she wasn't at all. In the military, family was family. But she had a feeling it was also a way of getting to know her… *friend*.

"Thank you, sir. I'll cover the damages to the machine and Christopher can pay me—"

"That's not acceptable. He did it; he will work it off."

"Uh, Dad, you might want to—"

"I'll do it," Christopher said from behind them while hugging the trash can. "It's okay. I'll do it."

"Well, if you two are done making eyes at each other, I suggest you take your son home. Oh four hundred comes early, especially when he'll be working here after school for the next few years to pay for that machine he broke."

Christopher moaned. *"Years?"*

Chapter 10

Grayson left Christopher in the truck and walked Frankie to her Jeep parked at the garage.

The moment they were out of viewing range, Grayson pressed her against the side of the vehicle and lowered his head, taking her mouth in a kiss that left them both breathing shakily by the time he lifted his head. "You are an amazing woman."

"Because I agreed to help with boot camp?"

"That and because you got your father to keep the police out of things," he said, kissing her once more. "The part, London's, now the pier house. I thought things would be different when we moved here. When I got him away from the crowd he was running with back in Charlotte."

"He's struggling to find his place, but you can do this. He needs structure. Discipline."

"He needs the fear of God put in him, but you do that these days and the parents wind up in jail."

"Thus, boot camp. You've got this," she said, palming his cheek and smiling when he turned his face into her hand.

"Text me when you get home so I know you made it safely."

"I'll be fine."

"Text me anyway," he ordered.

Frankie slid her hands up along his neck and behind his head.

"You're awfully bossy. Maybe I don't want to—"

He ended the complaint with two more kisses and then reluctantly pulled away. "No take-backs," he said. "But I would understand if you're not up for boot camp after a sleepless night." The last thing he wanted was to add more stress to her overly stressed life. He wanted to pamper her, help her heal.

"I'll be up. I rarely sleep past three."

Such a telling statement, that. He brushed the hair from her face and stared down into her sparkling eyes, rubbing his thumb lightly over her full lips. He wished he was there for her in the middle of the night when she was awake and sleep-less. Wished he could hold her and take the night-mares and images from her.

"You can do this, Grayson. He won't like it now, but later, when he isn't serving a prison sentence, he'll be grateful."

He kissed her one last time and forced himself to step away so he could open the door for her to climb in. The Jeep roared to life, and he watched as she drove away, the loud engine doing nothing to drown out the sound of Christopher dry heaving and then hurling in the backseat of his truck.

Grayson returned to the vehicle and grimaced at the smell emanating from the back. "You're going to clean that up," he said, slamming the door as hard as he could.

"Ow. Dad. My head hurts. I need medicine."

"Nah. You're not getting any. I'm going to let you feel every ounce of happiness you get from underage drinking and then… we're really going to have some fun."

AT 3:58 the next morning, Grayson entered Christopher's room and began banging two pots together. The clanging had Christopher jackknifing upright in his bed and then falling back against the wall, hands holding his head as he whimpered.

"Dad! Dad, stop!"

"Nope. Get dressed."

"What? *Why?*"

He banged the pots again and Christopher covered his ears. "Get dressed. Gym shorts, running shoes. You've got sixty seconds or you go barefoot in your boxers."

"Go where?"

"Fifty seconds." He banged the pots a few more times. "Forty."

"All right. *Stop*. My head."

Chris pulled on shorts and shoved his feet into his shoes but didn't tie them.

"What's wrong? Is there a fire?"

"There will be if you don't get going."

"What's wrong? What'd I do?"

"Think about it a second."

Christopher stared at Grayson a long moment before his expression began to change. "There you go. Yeah, you're in deep, too."

"Dad—"

"Save it. You are officially in boot camp," Grayson stated, using his ex-military outdoor voice because of the way it made Christopher cringe.

"You will do what I say, when I say, where I say, or the photos of you *stealing* items from London's Lattes, selling stolen property at the garage, and vandalizing and breaking the machine at the pier house will be added to what the cops already know of your underage drinking."

Christopher's eyes went wide.

"You don't remember the cops?"

"N-no."

"Ah, well, you made quite the show of yourself, which is why, if you don't do what I say, I'll let them charge you and you'll be punished by a judge. Do you understand?"

"Yeah, but… Dad, I'm sorry. And the part… I needed the cash for Cat's gift."

"Do you understand?" Grayson shouted.

Christopher groaned and held his head. "Owww! Yeah, whatever."

"Last night was a courtesy. From now on, you'll sleep in the spare bedroom."

"What? There's no furniture in there."

"This room is a privilege I am not required to offer. A mattress, food, clothing. Those you'll get, but privileges like in-room television and gaming systems must be earned. Things cost money, Chris. The items you keep stealing? Those were earned, but not by you. As of now you get what I give you."

"Dad—"

"Downstairs. Go."

Christopher took a wide berth as he passed by Grayson, but the kid still muttered under his breath.

"You will not complain," Grayson continued in his most authoritative voice. "You'll reap consequences for complaining on top of those you're receiving based on your recent *criminal* activities. You will be monitored at all times. School, work at the pier house to repay the debt you owe Mr. Cohen, chores here to repay me for the part you stole, and boot camp. Those are your activities. Your *only* activities."

"What? For how long?" Christopher stomped down the stairs. "What about Cat? We're supposed to go to the beach today."

"Maybe you should've thought of that before you turned into a delinquent. You won't have time to date. You'll be too busy working to pay off the damages. You don't work and you will be charged. Do you understand?"

They made it to the front door. Grayson opened it just as Frankie exited her Jeep in the driveway.

"I'm glad Mom took a bat to your stupid bike!

You wanted rid of her! That's why you *killed* her! You didn't want her anymore just like you don't want me!"

"I wouldn't be doing this if I didn't love you," Grayson growled. "I'm trying to keep you out of—"

"That's a lie! You don't want me. You're not even my real father, but you're stuck with me because she's dead! You hate me as much as *I hate you*!"

Shock rolled through him, sucking the breath from his lungs. "*Christopher, enough.*"

"Send me away! Call the police! See if I care!"

Frankie raced up the steps toward them. She met his gaze briefly and must have sensed what he couldn't say, because she turned Christopher to face her.

"If he wanted rid of you, the *easy* thing to do would be pressing charges," she said softly, calmly. "Not listen to you have a temper tantrum and whine because you got caught. Now shut up and run, and don't stop until we tell you to."

Christopher hesitated a long moment before he sobbed and stomped down the stairs. He walked to the sidewalk, but after a look over his shoulder, the teen broke into a slow jog.

"I… I didn't know he knew I wasn't…" Grayson

inhaled. "Daria said we'd tell him together one day, but as far as I knew…"

"It doesn't matter how he found out. You need to do damage control because now he feels he's been lied to his entire life. Let him calm down and then try to explain. Until then"—Frankie grasped Grayson's hand and pulled him toward the stairs—"we run and pray we can keep up with him. Angry kids run the fastest."

Chapter 11

A week into their morning boot camps, Frankie found herself alone with Christopher when Grayson got a call from work saying he needed to report for an emergency. She assured him she'd be okay, but she could tell Grayson was nervous about leaving her to face Christopher's anger and angst alone.

She kept pace with the kid for a while, but when it kept getting slower, she decided a little egging was in order. "You really gonna let a girl outrun you? Pick up the pace."

"I hate this. I should just let them take me away. He'd be happy then."

"If you really believe that, you're more clueless

than I thought." The early-morning sunrise was just beginning to lighten the sky in purple hues.

"Whatever."

"You don't believe me?"

"No. He's not my dad."

Grayson told her he'd tried multiple times to talk to Christopher over the course of the last week, but Christopher would rather sit in the empty spare bedroom staring at the walls than hear him out. "Look, kid, do you think he'd fight for you like he has if he didn't love you? Work so hard to keep you *out* of trouble with the police?"

Christopher huffed and puffed.

"He just doesn't want to look bad by getting rid of me."

"Uh-huh. Clueless. Word to the wise, kid, no one cares these days. Everyone has something they're dealing with whether it's sickness or jobs or kids in trouble. It would be *easy* for your dad to pawn you off, but that's not what good parents do. Do you know how hard it is to keep going when you aren't grateful? Thankful? When you spew hate more often than not? To get up in the morning and do *this* when he's got a super stressful job and a slew of other responsibilities where people's lives depend on him? That's love in action. Now pick up the pace."

"But—"

"Pick up the freaking pace!"

Christopher picked up speed as ordered and they fell into a more natural stride. The kid's endurance had increased dramatically in a short amount of time. After they sprinted to the halfway mark and turned to go back, Frankie said, "What do you know about that bike of his?"

Christopher cursed and Frankie ordered him to stop, drop, and give her twenty.

"What?"

"You will not use that kind of language around me or around my father's business and employees. *Drop.*"

Christopher glared at her and Frankie knew she was pushing him hard, but she was sick of hearing him complain and didn't want him to be the kid her father's customers talked about later.

And she could use the breather from the spasm in her side and twenty would give it.

The teenager glared at her and counted off the push-ups. When he finished, they started running again. "What do you know about your dad's bike?"

"Only that I'm glad my mom took a bat to it. He loves it more than he ever loved us."

Frankie shook her head. "Once again, clueless. Yeah, he loves that bike, but it's painfully obvious that you don't know why."

Christopher ran a ways in silence. "Tell me."

"Uh-uh. Not my story to tell but it's one you'll want to hear. So ask. Got it?"

They made the left turn onto K Avenue and headed toward the pier just as the sun was starting to truly crack the surface. "We're going to miss it. Beat me there and I'll buy you breakfast after we meet the colonel on the beach."

The boy kicked it up big-time and Frankie was no match for his long legs as he booked it toward the pier. Christopher was stretching and staring out at the water when she finally caught up.

"I want the works," he said, grinning at her with full-blown teen ego. "Bacon, eggs, waffles. Everything."

She leaned her hands on her thighs and bent, trying to catch her breath. "Yeah, yeah. But now that I know what you can do, that pace is going to get faster even if I have to ride a bike beside you to keep up."

• • •

THAT EVENING, Grayson knocked on Frankie's door and waited, flowers in hand. The door swung wide, and he smiled at the way her eyes widened at the surprise.

"Going to a funeral?"

He chuckled at her statement and dropped a kiss on her forehead before lowering his head to steal a kiss. "Brat. I'm sorry I left you to face his bad mood this morning."

"Yeah, well, that kid can run. You need to get him into track or cross country when all of this is over. I, um, didn't expect to see you."

"Your dad called and asked if Christopher could work, so I don't have guard duty." He peered over her shoulder, frowning when he spotted Tank's dog bowl on the floor beside the coffee table with a spoon in it. Tank sat by the bowl, licking his chops. "Is this a bad time? What's happening here?"

"Hmm? Oh, nothing."

Somehow he didn't think that was nothing. "You going to take these?" Grayson handed over the flowers and watched as Frankie paused to take a sniff before moving to the kitchen. She found a vase and put them in water before moving to join him on the couch.

"How's the patient?"

"Okay now." He shifted to lean sideways, facing her. "How was your day?" He liked this. This seemingly unimportant important conversation that couples had every day. Frankie might argue their conversation was *friendly*, but he'd take this in whatever form it came in.

"Got some new business today, which is always good. And I finally hired a new mechanic to replace the one I had to fire."

"Another vet?"

"You know it."

Something else to love about her. Frankie fiercely wanted to help those who'd served their country and returned to find jobs had been lost, or those who struggled with PTSD symptoms and struggled to keep afloat because of it. It was something the colonel had mentioned in passing several times as only a proud papa could. "You sleeping?" he asked, brushing his thumb gently over the shadows beneath her eyes.

"Ah, Dr. Grayson is in the house."

"I'm no doctor, just a concerned boyfriend."

Her dark eyebrows rose. "Boyfriend, you say? As in you're a boy and a friend?"

"For now," he said, letting her think whatever

she needed to so long as it kept conversations like this one going. He slid his hand along her neck and gently tugged her toward him, brushed his lips over hers while holding her gaze. "Until I can get you to agree to more."

Wariness flashed over her features, but he refused to let it daunt his determination. He sealed his lips over hers, relishing the hitch in her breathing and the tiniest of moans she released when he deepened the kiss. "Come here."

Tank grumbled from where he sat nearby. Grayson ignored the dog, but when Tank went on a minute-long grumbling spree that left Frankie groaning, he ended the kissing and turned his irritation to the dog. "Yes, I'm macking on your girl. What's the problem?"

Another low grumble from Tank left them both laughing.

"Ignore him. He's hungry."

Grayson eyed the bowl full of food. "So why doesn't he eat?"

Frankie groaned and tried to bury her head, but the blazing color filling her face had Grayson pulling away to see the sight and determine the source. "What?"

"It's awful. You'll *laugh*."

"After this week, I need a good laugh. And you are crazy adorable when you blush. I don't think I've ever seen you do that."

"Stop it."

"Why won't he eat?"

"Because… he wants me to feed him."

"Feed him?" Grayson stared at her, not comprehending until he looked back at the bowl and spotted the spoon once more. "You mean you actually…?"

Frankie burrowed her head into his chest as Grayson laughed so hard he shook the couch. She lightly punched him and he laughed harder, squeezing her tight and burying his smile in her hair. His rough, tough, military brat and mechanic girlfriend was a total pushover when it came to her highly trained war dog. It gave him hope that he'd wear her down and she'd forgive him completely for being an utter fool.

"Stop already. I know it's crazy."

He kissed her head, her cheek, stole another kiss from her lips before he pushed her away. He grabbed the bowl from the floor so he could slide off the couch and then pulled her down beside him. "I have to see this."

"You can't tell anyone. *Ever*."

He handed her the bowl and watched as she hefted the spoon in Tank's direction.

Grayson knew he would've fallen in love with her in that moment... if he wasn't already.

Chapter 12

Grayson rolled over in bed and glared at the alarm. Three fifty-eight. It was Thanksgiving Day and they were due at his aunt and uncle's house at noon. Frankie had agreed to join his family for their meal, but Grayson refused to overthink the fact that it was the colonel who had invited Grayson and Christopher to join the Cohens for dinner at six and not his stubbornly silent girlfriend.

Frankie was obviously holding back and he understood her reservations, but his goal of wearing down her defenses meant discovering unusual ways of going about it. She wasn't a normal woman and he loved that about her. But it also made breaking through more difficult.

The buzzer blared and he groaned. Sleeping in

seemed like a really good thing. He was getting too old for this, but there was something to be said for leading by example, and like the colonel had said, it was a great way of spending quality time with Christopher.

Grayson smashed the button to silence it and rolled upright, sliding his feet into shoes he'd left out the night before while grabbing the shirt and shorts from the end of the bed. Seconds later he opened the door to find Christopher standing outside, mid-stretch.

"About time. I thought I was going to have to find the pots."

Grayson smirked and did a few stretches of his own. "You're getting into this."

Christopher shrugged but the move wasn't as casual as his son tried to make it seem.

"I'm doing better in gym class. The coach has said a few things."

"The girls at school are probably noticing, too," Grayson added, trying to boost the kid's ego.

"Yeah. Kinda makes up for Cat dumping me."

They headed downstairs and Grayson locked up behind them. "You ever going to tell me what happened?" Frankie wasn't there in the driveway and Grayson frowned. Should he text her? Sleep was a rare commodity for her, and he didn't want to wake her by texting if her phone wasn't on Do Not Disturb.

"She's one of those girls."

"What do you mean?"

Christopher shrugged and broke into a slow jog and Grayson fell into step beside him.

"She's... I don't know. It was stupid. Me bashing the machine at the pier house because of her. She'd gotten all of those presents at her party, but when she saw the prize in the machine, she had to have it, too, and said she'd... do stuff with whoever got it for her."

"Do stuff? She was your girlfriend."

"Supposed to be, but then the other guys there started trying to get it and... It was stupid."

Grayson whistled. How old was that girl to be behaving like that? "That's a tough lesson to learn, bub. I'm sorry that happened to you."

"Me, too. But I don't want to be with someone like that."

"Good. You deserve to be with someone who respects and honors what's between you. And you have plenty of time to meet a girl who will."

They jogged for a ways in silence.

"I know who they were now. Mom's... friends."

Grayson felt like someone had sucker-punched him. He struggled to breathe and keep pace at the announcement, but given the long-overdue talk, he found himself thankful Frankie wasn't there.

"I didn't at first. They'd play ball with me sometimes and she said… they came to look out for us because you were gone. That's why they were always around."

Grayson felt Christopher's embarrassment in talking about his mother's behavior. He kept his head straight, eyes on the road in front of them. One step in front of the other.

"I hated you when I realized she was… I thought you made her do that. I mean, if you'd have come home…"

"Chris—"

"But I get it now. Guess I can thank Cat for that. Mom…" Christopher's voice broke and thickened. "You took care of us even though you weren't around. She didn't have to do what she did with all those men."

All those men? Just how many were there?

Don't go there.

"All that matters now is that you know your mother loved you. What she did is in the past." It took a lot to say the words without the bitterness he'd felt creeping in, but now that he and Frankie were building a relationship, it was easier than it had been before.

"Frankie said I should ask you about the bike. Why you love it so much."

Silence followed the words, and it took Grayson six strides to get himself together enough to speak. Frankie… The woman had an insight he only dreamed of. If there was ever an appropriate time for Christopher to hear that story, it was now. "I got the bike from my dad. He died of cancer when you were just a baby."

"I don't remember him much."

"I know. It was a long time ago."

"So that's it? It was your dad's?"

"No. That's not it. I met the man I called my dad when I was eight years old."

Chris stopped running and Grayson slowed, turning to face his son on the road.

"You mean Grandpa wasn't—"

Grayson shook his head. "My biological father ran out on my mom and me. Up until then I'd spent my life watching him hit and abuse her. Grandpa was one of the cops who'd come to the house that last time. He'd check up on us every now and again, see how we were doing, and about a year or so later, they got married. He raised me, taught me integrity, honor, respect. Everything."

"Did you always know I wasn't yours?"

Grayson nodded. "Your mother was pretty far along before we got together. I was overseas when she conceived, but I'm on your birth certificate. We agreed that we'd tell you one day, but we thought it might be best to wait until you were older."

"I heard people talking at the funeral. I felt stupid."

He could only imagine how that had made Christopher feel, and Grayson kicked himself for not realizing the source sooner. "I'm sorry. The choice wasn't made to hurt you, Chris, but for us to be father and son."

Christopher inhaled and started walking away, then jogging. Grayson moved to catch up.

"I'm sorry I took the part. I shouldn't have stolen it."

"You're not the same person now you were then. You've changed a lot since that happened. I see that. I hope you see that, too."

"I do. I feel… different."

"Good. And apology accepted." Grayson saw the impact of his words on Chris, how his son lifted his chin a little higher, his expression a little more confident.

"Frankie's nice."

"I agree."

"She's a pain when she's in boot-camp mode though."

Grayson laughed and nodded. "She's one of a kind, that's for sure."

"What happened to her?"

Grayson turned his head toward his son. "What do you mean?"

"The scars on her belly?"

"I… didn't know she had scars."

"Oh." Christopher looked uncomfortable. "Um… we were doing stretches and her shirt pulled up. I looked… but I didn't mean to," he added quickly. "But that's when I saw them."

Grayson kept running, back to forcibly putting one foot in front of the other even though he wanted to get to Frankie's as fast as possible to find out what had happened. He'd seen her in a bathing suit once in California when a group of them had gone to the beach for the day. She'd had no scars then. "You didn't mention them? She didn't?"

"No. I pretended I didn't see them. I hate that

she got hurt, though. They looked painful. You, um, want to sprint?"

That was all the warning Grayson got before Christopher took off and shot ahead of him. He had speed, and his endurance had really grown. Frankie was right, track or cross country would be a good fit for the kid.

Grayson picked up speed but his heart, his mind weren't on running.

Where had she gotten the scars?

One thing he knew for certain—he would find out. But how was he going to bring it up without her PTSD surfacing as well?

Chapter 13

Thanksgiving Day flew by with too much food and a strange tension in Grayson that Frankie couldn't place. She was late getting to his aunt and uncle's house for lunch because the first time she'd tried browning the marshmallows atop her sweet potato casserole, she'd burnt them instead. The second time was the charm—after doing a lot of repair work and a secret taste test to make sure nothing tasted charred. Cooking? Not her forte. But give her something mechanical and she could kick serious butt.

Grayson had tried to get her alone a few times, but something about his expression left her retreating and making excuses. Today wasn't the day to fight, and she had a feeling whatever it was on his mind would end up with them there.

Dinner at her parents' house had been even more tense because of London. Her sister had glared at her from across the table, even though Frankie had told London their father was the one responsible for him being there.

Not that she minded Grayson being there. It was actually nice sitting beside him and sharing a meal with her family. Nice to see him and Christopher joking and laughing with her father. It was only when he glanced at her with *that look* she couldn't decipher that she got nervous.

She'd made an excuse and driven herself to both meals because she wasn't prepared to go public with their couple status, especially when there was still an important conversation she needed to have with Grayson. Things were getting more and more serious by the day, the kissing hotter and hotter, and she knew they'd far surpassed the point where full disclosure should've occurred.

This time, however, she was the one keeping secrets. But to what end? If she told him and it changed things, well…

Grayson had asked to talk to her when he'd walked her to her Jeep, but she'd put him off with yet another excuse. She was exhausted, truth be told, and to have the conversation she needed to have meant doing so after a decent night's sleep. Maybe she should take the meds the doctor had prescribed, just once, to see if they helped her sleep an entire night? She'd stressed the Thanksgiving festivities to the point of not sleeping and then finally slept so deeply she'd slept through her alarm and boot camp.

Tank sank down on his haunches with a grumble, earning her attention. "Seriously? No, no, no. I'm not doing it tonight. I refuse to spoon-feed my *war-hero* dog. You need to get over yourself."

Tank lowered himself to the floor in front of his bowl but didn't take a bite. He looked at her with his big brown eyes and gave such a pitiful whine she felt herself wavering. "Eat. Now. Or I'll put *you* in boot camp and give those bolts and pins of yours a workout."

A knock sounded at her door, and she hesitated a long moment before shoving herself off the couch. She'd told Grayson she was tired and turning in early. Surely he wouldn't show up and—

"Frankie, open up."

Frankie swung the door wide to see London—

and the rest of her sisters standing shoulder to shoulder. Oh, so not good. "Uh, hello?"

London was the first to break ranks and, after a quick glance toward Frankie's flip-flopped feet, grabbed her apartment keys from the bowl where they were kept before taking Frankie's hand.

"Let's go."

"Go? Where?"

"We know you got the text to meet us but you didn't show."

"My DND is on." She might have turned on Do Not Disturb *after* seeing the text, but they didn't need to know that.

"You're not getting out of this," London said. "We're doing an intervention."

"An inter— Excuse me?"

"You've avoided us for weeks," Ireland stated, giving Frankie a baleful stare.

Tank pressed against her leg and she automatically reached down to stroke his head. "I'm *busy*. I do have a life and a business to run, you know."

"And a love life apparently. One involving a liar and a cheater," London said softly.

Frankie gasped. "You *promised* you wouldn't—"

"You need a sounding board and we're it," London said. "Or have you forgotten?"

She glared at London and wished they were kids again when she could sit on Londy and pull her hair. "You said I needed to know the whole story."

"For closure, yes. I didn't tell you to start things up again with someone known for lying to you and cheating on his wife."

"We didn't cheat. We didn't even kiss! I can't *believe* you told them."

"Don't blame Londy," Ireland said. "Grayson's obviously got Daddy on his side since he invited Grayson to our family dinner, but Daddy doesn't *know* your history with Grayson, does he?"

"Or that Grayson's the reason you almost got yourself killed," Holland added.

"Uh, guys," Carolina said.

"You have no business intruding into—"

"Guys?"

"Something that's—"

"Of course it's our business. You're our business."

"Guys?"

Everyone was talking at once but stopped at Carolina's urgent tone. Her sisters turned to look down the hallway, and a hard knot formed in Frankie's stomach.

"Am I interrupting?" Grayson asked from the hallway.

Oh, no. This was *not* how she wanted things to go down.

Frankie moved toward the door the same time that Grayson stepped behind her sisters, standing head and shoulders above them. "Grayson… hi."

Grayson's gaze didn't budge from hers, pain and wariness etched on his handsome features so deeply it rolled off of him.

"What does she mean I almost got you killed?"

Frankie cringed and sucked in a sharp breath. "You *didn't*."

"Liar."

"Londy, so help me, I will knock you *out* if you don't shut your—"

"Ladies, would you excuse us? Frankie and I need to talk."

Carolina crossed her arms over her front and glared at him.

"We're not going anywhere. You've hurt her enough."

Frankie closed her eyes and fisted her hands, thinking it really wouldn't be bad to be an only child. "Caro, leave. Now. All of you need to leave," she said to her sisters.

"No. We're not going anywhere," London said. "You—"

"Fine. Then *I'll* leave," she said, plowing through the wall of sisters to reach Grayson.

Without a word, Grayson handed the bag of food in his hand to Holland and fell into step beside her.

Frankie didn't stop walking until she'd stalked from the complex all the way to the beach. The sand was cold on her feet but it didn't matter. None of it mattered now. She was going to spend the rest of her life in prison for murder. What was the count for killing four sisters?

"Start talking."

She fisted her hands and stopped so fast sand flew up in the air. "You didn't almost get me killed."

"Where did the scars come from?"

She swung to face him. "What do you— I-I mean, how do you know about them?" She'd been careful. In all of the kissing and hand wandering, she'd never let him touch her under her clothes in case he felt them and asked questions she wasn't ready to answer.

"Christopher said he saw them one day. He asked me about them. What they're from. I had to admit I didn't know."

She turned away from him to face the surf, and he gently grasped her arm, tugging her around until she had no choice but to face him. "It happened in Kabul," she said simply. "After we— After I found out you were married, a buddy got sick and I volunteered to cover for him."

Grayson sucked in a breath, his eyes softening as awareness dawned. Just as quickly, a look of horror flashed.

"The bomb. Your PTSD. That's where it— *Frankie.*"

He reached down and tugged at her sweatshirt, and she slapped his hands away. "Stop it."

"Let me see."

"It's too dark and they're not important."

"Not impor— How bad was it? Your injuries? How bad?"

She tucked her chin to her chest and was glad they'd left the bright lights of her apartment. Here in the dark, on the beach, she had some privacy. "Internal bleeding, d-damage."

"What kind of damage?"

This. This was what she needed to tell him. Didn't want to tell him. Didn't want to have to admit, even to herself. "When I woke up they said I can't... I can't have kids now. I-I had to have a full hysterectomy."

Frankie felt his withdrawal before she experienced it. Grayson let go, took a step back. Two. He lifted his hands to his head and raked them over the top. "Grayson, it's not your fault."

"Of course it is."

"No, it's *not*. Muldoon was sick. Someone had to go."

"But you volunteered because of *me*. You almost *died* because of me!"

"No, I... I was a soldier. Someone had to take the duty and I—"

"I have loved and cared for two women, Frankie. Two. And I have managed to hurt *both* of them. How can you stand there and not want me dead after what I took from you?"

"You love me?"

A sound left him, carried away on the wind.

She stepped toward him, but at the same time, he swung away from her, giving her his back. "Grayson, it's not your fault. What will it take to convince you?"

"You can't."

"So that's it? You find me again, tell me you *love me*, and now you're done?"

He'd turned as though to walk back toward the complex but stopped, his head hanging low.

"I suppose I am."

"Grayson—"

"Your sisters are right, Frankie. I've taken enough of your life from you."

Frankie stood there and watched as Grayson stalked away. When she couldn't see him anymore, she sank to the sand, unable to bear the thought of going back inside to face the sister-fest waiting for her with all of their looks and I-told-you-so's.

The scent of Holland's perfume reached Frankie before she saw or heard them. Frankie closed her eyes, feeling them surround her one by one.

"Frankie?"

London. Frankie lifted her head and glared at her twin. "Happy now? He's gone."

"Frankie, that's not fair," Ireland said softly. "London's worried about you. We're all worried about you."

"Yeah, well, you don't need to worry anymore. Grayson blames himself. Even though," she said, glaring at London, "it wasn't his fault. Y'all always talk about divine plans and fate and all that, but apparently you don't listen to yourself."

"What do you mean?" Carolina said.

"I mean, if I'm meant to die or have kids or *not* have kids, it's going to happen because it's bigger than us, right? *So*... what about that?" A rough laugh left her. "I've forgiven Grayson. We were... It was *good*. He told me *loved me*."

"Oh, Frankie."

"But apparently he can't see past the guilt y'all piled on because he blames himself more than even you blame him," she said, getting to her feet despite the protests it brought. "Go home. You've done more than enough for tonight."

"Frankie, wait," Carolina called.

"Leave me alone. I need to *be* alone and... I have to go spoon-feed my freaking dog!"

Chapter 14

Frankie was elbow deep in an engine a few days later when she realized she wasn't alone.

"Frankie?"

She twisted her head and peered out from under the hood to see Christopher standing several feet away. "Hey. Aren't you supposed to be working at the pier house?"

"I'm going there now but... I wanted to say I'm sorry. I told Dad about the scars. On your stomach. I saw them one day and... I'm sorry. That was... private, I guess, huh?"

Apparently nothing in her life was private. "It's all good," she said, forcing a smile.

"You haven't been showing up for boot camp. And Dad's really grouchy. Did you break up?"

She inhaled and took a step back, straightening. "Yeah, I suppose we did. I... I'm going to work out on my own from now on, but if your dad can't go with you some mornings, text me and I'll meet you. Okay?"

"Yeah. I guess," Christoper said, unmoving.

The kid looked so sad, it tugged at her heartstrings, but after crying herself to sleep every night since that fight on the beach and enduring radio silence from Grayson, pretty much everything left her teary-eyed and angry. She refused to chase a man. Grayson had to come to terms and deal with what had happened to her, just like she'd had to. And if he couldn't...

She turned to move to her toolbox and dug around inside, not sure of what she searched for.

"Frankie?"

"Yeah."

"Can I ask a favor? A big favor?"

"I suppose it can't hurt to ask. No promises on doing it, though. What's up?" She held her breath, hoping the kid wasn't going to ask her to go to Grayson and talk about something, because seeing him face-to-face right now would shred what was left of her heart.

"It's just... Christmas is coming up, and I don't

have any money to get him anything. I asked Dad about his bike, though, and he told me the story about Grandpa. Dad's got all the parts, I think. So I was wondering if maybe you'd help me fix it? I can't pay you, but once I work off the machine I broke at the pier house, I could work here. There's got to be something I could do."

She stared into Christopher's hopeful face and sighed. "You've put some thought into this."

"I really want to fix it. Mom shouldn't have— It's important and I owe it to my dad for being my dad when he doesn't have to be."

"Christopher, your father loves you whether you're biologically his or not."

"I know. But I want to make up for being a jerk. Will you help me? I thought I could ask the colonel to cover for me. Say he needed me more hours, then I could come here instead. It's a lie, but it's just until the bike is fixed, and it's a surprise, you know?"

"You do realize the colonel and I would both be keeping track of you on those days. One miss and you'd be in trouble."

"I'll be here. I promise."

She stacked her arms over her chest and stared at him, knowing she didn't have the heart to say no. "You got a plan for getting the bike here?"

"Yeah. It's been covered up in the garage since we moved, so I thought I could come up with something to make it look like the bike's still underneath, but bring the real one here. I know it's a lot to ask, especially since you're not dating now, but will you help me?"

Frankie stared at Christopher a long moment before she nodded. "It'll take some doing, but, yeah, I'll help you fix it. There's a parts bike in the back you can use to put under the cover for now, too."

"Really?"

She nodded, smiling because of his excitement. "Text me sometime when he's not home and we'll figure out a time to make the swap. Now go get to work before you get busted for not being where you're supposed to be."

Christopher grinned and surged forward, wrapping his arms around her. He hugged her tight, the angry kid he used to be slowly changing into one more aware of those other than himself.

"Thank you."

"You got it," she said, releasing him. "Now go before the colonel sends out a search and retrieval team."

"Yes, ma'am."

Chapter 15

Frankie and Christopher managed to get the bike out of the garage without being caught, and as Christmas approached far too rapidly, she dedicated even more hours to repairing the Harley so Christopher could give his father the gift. The teen had a knack for mechanics and picked up on things quickly, but the repairs took time, and to get it finished meant working on it alone. She didn't mind, though. Well, not much. Not when she knew how much the bike meant to Grayson and now Christopher because of what it stood for.

The next two weeks flew by. Between her days at the garage, her evenings with Christopher, and the heartbreak that felt like a stone weighing her down, Frankie dragged through the days and fell into bed at night, exhausted.

Sometimes she wondered why she bothered working so hard on the project when Grayson hadn't contacted her since that night, but deep down she knew. Little good it did her.

Only she would fall in love with the man—again—only to get her heart broken. Again.

Her phone chimed and she glanced at the face.

We're almost home.

She glanced at Tank where he lay on the couch in her office and moved to pet the dog. "I'll be back soon, okay? Don't open your Christmas present without me."

CHRISTOPHER RAN the last few feet before turning to face Grayson.

"Remember what you said about us being honest with each other about everything? Not keeping secrets?"

Grayson felt his muscles tighten. "Yeah. Why? Chris, did you get into trouble again?"

"What? No. But Frankie is."

"She's in trouble? What's wrong?"

"She's sad, like hard-core sad."

"She said something to you?" He'd picked up his cell to call or text her a dozen times since their conversation on the beach, but something always stopped him. The fear of hurting her again after taking so much from her, the intimidating presence of her family and what would be their involvement in whatever future he might have with Frankie. The saying one married the family and not just the girl was true, and with Frankie's *four* sisters hating him because he'd practically shoved her on that convoy…

"No, but I thought you liked her? Loved her?"

"Christopher, it's complic—"

"Complicated. Yeah, that's what Frankie said, too. But why is it so complicated if you love each other? Isn't that enough?"

Grayson motioned for Chris to head home and fell into step beside him, walking to cool down. "It's not that simple. She made a decision because of me, one that got her severely injured and almost killed. Now she can't have kids and I'm responsible for that. I took that from her. You understand?"

"No. I mean, it's bad, but the colonel says when

soldiers sign up, they know what they're getting into. Are you saying she didn't?"

"No. That's not what I'm saying."

"But you said she did it because of you like she didn't make the decision on her own. She's got a Purple Heart. Does that mean she shouldn't?"

"What? No, not at all."

"Good. Because I don't think she would've gone just because you hurt her feelings."

"Chris, I didn't mean to imply—"

"Because it's about duty, right? She did her duty as a soldier and helped her friend by taking his place."

"That's right."

"So why is it your fault?"

"Because it just is."

"How?"

"She can't have kids now, Chris. She was hurt that badly, and even though she made the decision to go, I still feel responsible."

"That's stupid. Well, it is," Chris said with a shrug when Grayson sent him a fatherly glare. "If you had gone and been hurt, would you blame Frankie?"

"No. Of course not."

"Then why do you blame you when she doesn't?"

It was way too early to be having this conversation, Christmas morning or not. "Chris, I don't want to hurt her any more."

"But you love her."

"Yes, okay? I do. I love Frankie and it's because I love her and feel responsible for her getting hurt that I think it's best if I stay away."

"But that's *stupid*. I thought adults were supposed to be smart?" Chris kicked a rock in the road. "Frankie can't have kids, and you feel bad about it. So you're saying adopted kids aren't real kids?"

Had. He'd been *had*. Set up by a teenager too smart for his own good.

"Because *you said* blood doesn't matter."

"It doesn't."

"So if she doesn't blame you, and blood doesn't matter, what's the problem? If you feel so bad about hurting her, don't. Go make her happy again by loving her back like you say you do."

Grayson tucked his head to his chest as the impact and depth of Christopher's words sank in. Could it be that easy? Was he making a fool of himself again by not honoring Frankie's feelings—and his own—and moving forward instead of living in the past with things that couldn't be undone?

"Dad, if I asked for something for Christmas and it's the only thing I want, would you do it?"

"It's Christmas morning, bub. It's a little late for last-minute shopping."

"You don't have to shop for this. Just… talk to Frankie. Carolina told me the story about how you and Frankie keep meeting up with each other. Isn't that cool?"

"It is."

"Then how many times does it have to happen before you get why it's happening?"

Grayson inhaled and clamped a hand on Chris's shoulder. How many times, indeed. Hadn't he said basically the same thing to Frankie when they'd met up in Carolina Cove? "I think it just sank in. Thank you. Let's get inside and see if Santa showed, shall we?"

"Wait."

Christopher glanced at his cell phone and then down the street.

"What's going on?"

His son grinned. "We have to wait on your Christmas present."

Grayson stared down the street but didn't see anything. "Do, uh, I want to know how you paid for this present?"

"Dad, seriously?"

Grayson held up his hands in surrender and stood patiently, following Christopher's anxious stare to take in the empty, quiet street. A few lights were coming on at the neighbors' houses as people woke up, but there was nothing unusual happening that drew notice.

Nothing… except a low rumble in the distance. Christopher grinned and shifted his stance, turning so that he stared at Grayson.

The rumble grew louder and the single light on the front of the motorcycle grew brighter the closer it got to them. Grayson sucked in a sharp breath, glancing at the closed garage door and back at the bike slowing to turn into their drive.

Frankie.

"Which one of them is the present?" he asked Christopher, throat tight and choked at the sight of the woman he loved and the bike he loved both there like… like it was Christmas morning and his wish rolled up in one.

"Do you like it? I had to lie. I wasn't working at the pier house all the time like I said, but with

Frankie fixing the bike. Do you like your surprise?"

The air whooshed from his lungs and he stood there, completely overcome, because while he'd been so *stupid* and keeping his distance from Frankie out of some sort of twisted honor, she had been working with Christopher to restore something precious to him. Loving him despite his stupidity.

"Dad?"

"I love it," he said, barely able to get the words out over the lump in his throat. "Both of them." He released his hold on Chris's shoulder and stumbled forward. Frankie was in the process of lowering the kickstand, but he gripped her shoulder and tilted her head up to face him. He could see the wariness in her eyes and vowed he'd never put it there again. "I don't know what I did to deserve you," he said, lowering his head to kiss her but stopping just short of her mouth, "but I will spend the rest of my life loving every part of you if you'll give me the chance."

She lowered her lashes over her eyes and smiled. "It's about time you came to your senses."

He sealed his lips over hers and kissed her so long they grossed Christopher out and he announced he was going inside to check out his presents.

Grayson chuckled and ended the embrace. "You are an amazing woman."

"Oh, yeah? Combat boots and all?"

He stroked his thumb over her lip, following the movement with his eyes. "One day soon that's all you're going to wear for me."

"Mmm," she said, sighing the sound against his mouth. "Merry Christmas."

He tugged her off the bike and tucked her to his side. "Come on. I have a present for you."

"You do?"

He'd kept his mother's jewelry in a safe in the house, and he couldn't imagine anyone but Frankie wearing it. He didn't have a ring to give her—yet—but there was a diamond pendant on a silver chain he couldn't wait to place around her neck as a promise of what was to come now that they both finally realized their love was worth the risk.

Want to read more about the Cohen sisters? Read a short excerpt of Holland's story LOST LOVE FOUND:

Holland's heart pounded in her chest the entire walk to the elevator and the ride to the third floor. Which was crazy because she wasn't a young girl getting asked to sit at the lunch table with her first crush. At thirty-three, dating wasn't new. It was the fact this wasn't a date but she could easily see herself saying yes to Max should he ask. That was the issue, because she'd turned down the last couple of invitations she'd received due to sheer lack of interest.

She rushed into her room and stripped down, wishing she hadn't crumpled up the blouse she'd had on earlier. The pants were salvageable but she didn't want to look like she was trying too hard. So why was she? He was bored, passing the time in a houseful of women, and she was the only one relatively close to him in age. It wasn't interest that had drawn the invitation but necessity, unless he planned to spend the remainder of the evening alone or go out for some fun on an island not yet awakened by the summer tourist season.

She rummaged through the drawers holding the clothes she'd brought with her and found a pair of leggings. Thankfully she'd brought a super-soft turquoise top. Was she trying too hard not to impress? Tough call. But she didn't want to look frumpy, either.

"Ugh, why is this so difficult?" she muttered, yanking on the leggings and donning the shirt, because with all of her debating, she wasted precious time. Dressed, she went to the bathroom. Her hair was best left braided until she could wash out the salt, but she did a light touch-up on her mascara and lip gloss and deemed herself as passable.

Her phone chimed and glanced at the screen. Ireland.

Heard you scored a local assignment. Doing okay?

Yes. Fine. Heading downstairs to schmooze a bit.

After all, Ireland didn't need to know specifics. Or that Max had nothing to do with the job itself.

Fun! Any single, good-looking men involved?

Her sister would have to ask that question, wouldn't she? Ever since Ireland had fallen in love again, she'd been on a mission to set Holland up with one of her husband's friends, but thankfully the timing had never worked out.

Client is 92. Enough said, she texted back. Because if she opened the door by mentioning a super-sexy, presumably single Max, Holland knew she'd probably have to answer a bevy of texts from all of her sisters instead of heading downstairs to get to know the man in question.

She left her phone behind in her room and

made her way to the elevator, all too aware of that pulse-racing thing repeating itself on the way down to the lower level. She heard the billiard balls clanking together as she approached the room, and when she walked inside, Max racked them.

"Heard the elevator," he said simply.

"So I see."

"You any good?"

"We'll have to find out." It had been weeks since she'd played, but she and all of her sisters were good at the game thanks to way too many hours on bases with little to do and a father determined his girls would be able to hold their own in a male-driven world.

"You break."

Mmm. He was playing the gentleman, giving her the advantage. It could help. Because while she wasn't a man-trashing feminist, she refused to deliberately lose just because it might bruise his ego. She also had a feeling Max was the type of man who'd be able to tell if she threw the game, which meant a fifty-fifty chance of him losing respect for her for doing so.

She chose a cue and chalked up, forcing herself to take a breath and slow her heart rate. Steady hands were needed.

Holland did a few practice slides of the cue and exhaled slowly once more before letting the cue strike. The crack of sound seemed deafening, and she worried that she might have disturbed Violet upstairs, but given the size of the house, it undoubtedly wasn't an issue.

Several balls hit the pockets and she had a choice. "Solids." She'd always looked better in solids than stripes.

As she moved around the table and chose her next target, she felt Max's eyes on her.

"I get the feeling you're better at this than you let on."

His words brought a curl to her lips and she lined up her shot. And got it.

Max chuckled, the sound wry.

"Glad I didn't make a bet with you on this."

Mmm. That could be interesting. "It's not too late."

His gaze narrowed on her.

"That sounds like a challenge. What do you have in mind?"

CONTINUE READING LOST LOVE FOUND, THE FIFTH BOOK IN THE SEASIDE SISTERS SERIES! HAPPY READING!

THE SEASIDE SISTERS SERIES:

THE LAST GOODBYE

LATTES AND LULLABYES

MAP OF DREAMS

WORTH THE RISK

LOST LOVE FOUND

BONUS CONTENT:
Excerpt of Seascapes and
Vegas Mistakes

Chapter 1

Hey, I can tell you're exhausted from your week in Vegas but what's up with you?" Amelia asked, sliding Izzy a searching glance from the driver's seat. "I thought you'd be bouncing off the walls with excitement."

Isabel Shipley—Izzy to her friends and family—lifted a hand to rub her upper chest and wondered if it was time to break down and take something for the anxiety plaguing her ever since waking up in her hotel room this morning on her last day in Las Vegas.

The rumpled bed had said a lot of things, but it was the running shower and suddenly pounding head that wouldn't allow her to put two and two together and come up with anything other than sheer panic. Especially when a glance at the bedside clock gave her barely an hour to get to the airport and through Vegas security for her flight back home to Carolina Cove, North Carolina.

Given her frantic state to get out while the gettin' was good, she'd scrambled into clothes she'd purposely left out because she *always* ran late and grabbed the suitcase she had haphazardly packed the day before on a break from the gallery. After a last horrified glance at the open bathroom door and the scrumptiousness she left behind, she'd made a run for the hills and hopefully the return of her sanity.

She didn't *do* things like this. Ever.

So why had she?

Adrenaline had given her just enough mindfulness to hail a taxi, but the TSA line was long and she'd had to freaking *run* for her gate, arriving mere seconds before the door to the plane shut behind her as the last one to board.

Head throbbing from the stress ice pick stabbing her brain, she'd curled up against the window, her mind racing with questions and embarrassment as memories of the previous night surfaced until she fell into a fitful doze that came from too much stress, not enough sleep, a physical soreness that brought a blush to her cheeks.

Hours after leaving the hotel room and Vegas behind, her mind still hadn't come up with any logical answers. Truthfully, she couldn't even blame the champagne she'd drunk.

She'd only had three glasses over a span of time, but her excitement and adrenaline had known no bounds. And what better way to celebrate the completion of her first *real* showcase than with a tall, dark, and very gorgeous man?

He'd made her tingle. Like, seriously, *tingle*. She hadn't known such a thing was possible. Even more amazing, he'd seemed genuinely interested in her art and process, which was *such* a turn-on itself.

He also knew her cousin Michael and had attended her showcase because of it—which made him safer than the average Joe.

"Izzy? Seriously, you're worrying me. What's up?" her best friend asked.

Izzy watched as Amelia ran a hand over her rapidly expanding belly in a soothing-mama gesture and swallowed hard. She had to snap out of it. If anyone should be freaking out, it was Amelia. She was the one with twins on the way.

Izzy nodded to herself. *Suck it up, buttercup.* What

was done was done. She and Everett had flirted, sipped luscious champagne, played blackjack and… made a bet. Which was how she'd wound up listening to the shower spray in the next room.

Winner gets a kiss, he'd said.

Loser has to— "I-I...I'm fine. Just really, *really* tired." Because while her challenge hadn't been anything outrageous, it *had* led to the aftermath.

"But your show was a success? You texted and said you'd scored some good commissions and would text me later to tell me details."

Thankful for the distraction, Izzy turned her attention to the passing scenery. "Yeah, sorry about that. I went to the bar for a drink and...talked to friends."

Friend, rather. That's where she'd met him again. The handsome not-so-stranger who'd wandered through the gallery around each of her paintings as though looking over a Monet or something equally amazing. Everett had introduced himself as a long-time friend of her cousin Michael's, said that he'd seen her name on the signs about the gallery show, and remembered Michael bragging about his talented artist cousin and the timing of her upcoming show.

They'd chatted briefly, her entire body

humming with excitement because he was so...*so fine.*

But it wasn't until later when she'd met up with him in the bar that things had gone from casual conversation to major flirtation.

"I thought as much. You know, sometimes it really comes down to the people you know, which is why it's so important to get out there. So? Tell me. Who bought your work? Anyone famous?"

Izzy frowned. She'd stayed so busy in Las Vegas prepping for the show after the last-minute inclusion that she hadn't had time to miss home. But now that she was here?

The familiar sights and traffic signs pointing to Carolina Cove brought tears to her eyes and comfort to her soul.

Or maybe it was the relief that she could almost shut herself inside her apartment and pretend the last twelve hours hadn't happened?

Or relive them.

To be honest, it was a toss-up as to which she'd prefer.

How could a thirty-two-year-old woman get herself into such a pickle?

God forbid she ever admit this, but maybe her

mother was right? She was too old for this. The games that came with dating and…

It's not dating when it's a one-night stand.

Which she didn't do.

Ever.

Except with someone Michael knows?

Her cousin wasn't a saint by any means, but she was pretty sure he wouldn't want to go to a business meeting and find out what had happened to his "kid cousin" in Vegas. And if memory served, Michael and Everett were currently working on a project.

Great. Oh, great.

"Iz?"

She had to really focus to remember Amelia's question. "Um, I-I don't know. The buyers finalized everything with the curator. I'll get more details this week, I'm sure. There...wasn't much time there at the end." Because she'd finished the show floating on a cloud, having made plans to meet Everett to celebrate the completion.

"Well, it's fantastic. I'm so proud of you," Amelia said, sliding Izzy another glance from across the way as she crossed the bridge toward Carolina Cove.

"Thanks. I mean, they could always change their mind but—"

"No buts. It's awesome and doubtful that would happen, so accept the sales as a win. I'm happy for you."

"Yeah. It's just...surreal." *In so many ways.*

She appreciated Amelia's support. Her friend was the best, softhearted and understanding and supportive even though Izzy's crazy ideas weren't always thought through.

"Okay, so, you're only minutes away from home. Take today off to recoup and rest, and then you can hit the ground running tomorrow."

"Yeah, I think I might." Sleep was good. It would bring clarity. Right? Maybe then she could figure out exactly how she'd gone from being a not-so-wild child to waking up with a virtual stranger.

She'd had boyfriends. Two long-term ones and a handful of wannabes. But despite what people— especially her mother—might believe about artists and her so-called bohemian lifestyle, she wasn't a casual hookup kind of girl.

And other than talking and laughing and kissing —a *lot*—she wasn't sure when the scales had tipped during the night. Only that she'd allowed Everett to walk her to her hotel room in the wee hours of the morning after all their fun—and then invited him inside.

"Thanks again for picking me up."

"Absolutely. The timing couldn't have worked out better. I can drop you off and head to the film location to look around and still make it home early. I want to do something special for Lincoln's birthday. Especially since this is our last birthday alone for a while."

Izzy watched as Amelia slid her hand over her pregnant belly again and loved how happy her friend seemed to be. Pregnancy definitely agreed with her. "Good thing I have my sunglasses on," she teased. "You're absolutely glowing."

Amelia laughed, her earrings brushing her shoulders as she shrugged.

"I feel like it. I mean, it's weird but I have all of this *energy*. I'm told it's not the norm and usually the opposite is true, but I think I could climb mountains with energy to spare."

Izzy thought of how tired her older sister, Allie, had been during her pregnancies and shook her head. Definitely not the norm. "Just don't overdo it," Izzy said, wishing she could borrow some of that energy right now. Maybe then she wouldn't feel as though she'd been dragged out to sea by a riptide and been swimming against the current for days.

"Oh, I won't. I couldn't if I wanted to. Lincoln

has been waiting on me hand and foot when I get home from work, and no one on set will let me lift a finger. Oh! Crap."

"What?"

"Well, before I forget...I ran into the Babes while you were gone."

"And?"

"I hate to say it, but your mom *insists* we use her house for the baby shower you're hosting. I hope that's okay? When I told them we were going to have it downstairs at London's Lattes, the Babes... well, they made it *really* hard to say no."

No doubt they had. The Babes rarely took no for an answer to anything. But why should they when the five older women had been catered to their whole lives?

During the summers of '58 and '59, four prominent Carolina Cove neighbors and friends had given birth to baby girls. One even had a set of twins. The proud mothers had taken the babes for daily strolls in their prams—and the locals had nicknamed them the Boardwalk Babes—a name used to this day by the now sixty-somethings.

All in all, Izzy had four pseudo aunts and ten "cousins," seven female and three male—with the twin Babes each having a set of twins of their own

—ranging in age from mid-forties all the way down to Izzy's thirty-two. Growing up, it had sucked to always be the youngest. Even more so because not only had her two older sisters treated her like the baby but all of her "cousins" had as well. She'd always been the kid sister no one wanted tagging along to dampen their fun.

"Okay," Amelia said, turning down the street toward London's Lattes and pulling to a stop behind Izzy's VW Bug convertible. Betty the Bug might be old, but she was still just as pretty as the day Izzy had bought her. Minus a little sun damage the south was known for.

"Need help getting in?" Amelia asked.

"No. I've got it. Thanks."

Izzy had rented the apartment above the coffee shop a little over a year ago when London Cohen, owner of London's Lattes, had met and then married a northern transplant who'd moved to the beach with his adopted children. Making rent wasn't always easy with her sporadic sales, but there was no denying being on her own gave Izzy a sense of freedom and independence she'd longed for after far too many years under her parents' roof.

Living a minimalist lifestyle made it easier to live sale to sale, but it didn't leave much in the bank afterwards. Not that her parents needed to know that. But thankfully with her commissions from the Vegas showcase, she now had a cushion that would allow her to breathe for at least six months. She would put that time to good use.

Her mother had never understood why Izzy felt the need to move out of their garage apartment into an apartment several blocks away, but Izzy knew if she ever had a hope of proving her abilities and worth, she had to stand on her own. Even if it meant giving up more than a few luxuries. Life was about more than just things. It was experiences and moments...moments she captured and painted because she couldn't imagine doing anything else with her life—no matter what her family said.

"Okay, so get in there and get some rest. You don't seem like yourself, and you'll need all the energy you can muster now that the Babes are involved in the baby shower. I have a feeling things might be a little over-the-top now."

"Ain't that the truth," Izzy muttered, pulling her lips into a wry twist of dread. If her mother and the rest of the Babes knew one thing, it was how to entertain. Nothing could be simple. A party—especially a baby shower welcoming a new life into the world—would be "Babe-ified" in the extreme.

"Sorry. I know I should've protested more, but you know how they can be."

"Trust me, I know," Izzy said truthfully. "And it's not a problem. I'm used to dealing with my mother and the Babes. No worries." While navigating the Babes might make shower prepping more stressful, Izzy wouldn't be responsible for footing the bill on the Babes' many additions to the planning. If nothing else, that was a win for her in a time when she needed to bank and save as much as she could for a rainy day.

"Iz?"

Izzy was halfway out the door when Amelia stopped her. "Yeah?"

"What's with the ring? You're pretty eclectic but that's not exactly your usual style," Amelia said with a wry expression and a little laugh.

Izzy glanced down at the gaudy, sparkling double dice ring she wore on the ring finger of her left hand. One she'd thought about taking off on the plane but hadn't because of the memories it now held in the somewhat sensual-coated space in her brain from last night.

The fun of three glasses of bubbly seemed like a good idea while she had such a great time with a handsome, charismatic man. "Oh, it's just, um, a souvenir," she said, swallowing hard because of the way her heart began to pound in her chest when an image appeared in her mind. The champagne-coated edges of her memories sharpened, and she zeroed in on the moment her gorgeous companion had slid the ring onto her finger, a smile on his seductive lips that she'd matched with one of her own.

"Good thing. For a second there I thought you'd gone and gotten married in Vegas."

Izzy released a laugh that sounded shriller than she'd intended and slid her purse to her shoulder. "You know how it goes. What happens in Vegas stays in Vegas."

SEASCAPES AND VEGAS MISTAKES

Books Also Set in Carolina
Cove

CAROLINA COVE SERIES:

- SEASCAPES AND VEGAS MISTAKES
- SEASHELLS AND WEDDING BELLS
- SEA GLASS AND SECOND CHANCES
- SEA BLUE AND LOVING YOU
- SEA VIEW AND SOMETHING NEW

MAKE ME A MATCH SERIES:

- ROMANCE RESET
- RULES OF ENGAGEMENT

- THE MATCHMAKER'S SECRET
- PERFECTLY MISMATCHED
- BY THE BOOK

THE SEASIDE SISTERS SERIES:

- THE LAST GOODBYE
- LATTES AND LULLABYES
- MAP OF DREAMS
- WORTH THE RISK
- LOST LOVE FOUND

COMING SOON: (LINKS WILL BE UPDATED ASAP)
THE BLACKWELL BROTHERS SERIES:

- BABY BE MINE
- SECOND CHANCE WEDDING
- THE GETAWAY GUY
- OFF-LIMITS LOVE
- FLIRTING WITH FOREVER

Also by Kay Lyons

MONTANA SECRETS SERIES:

- HEALING HER COWBOY
- IT HAD TO BE YOU
- HERS TO KEEP
- MILLION DOLLAR STANDOFF
- HIS CHRISTMAS WISH
- THEIR SECRET SON

THE SEASIDE SISTERS SERIES:

- THE LAST GOODBYE
- LATTES AND LULLABYES
- MAP OF DREAMS
- WORTH THE RISK
- LOST LOVE FOUND

TAMING THE TULANES SERIES:

- SMALL TOWN SCANDAL
- THEIR SECRET BARGAIN
- CROSSING THE LINE
- THE NANNY'S SECRET
- SOMEONE TO TRUST

THE STONE RIVER SERIES:

- WORTH THE WAIT
- NOT BY SIGHT
- THROUGH THE VALLEY
- LEAD ME NOT
- CHRISTMAS AT HOLLY WOOD
- THEIR CHRISTMAS MIRACLE
- SECOND CHANCES

SMALL TOWN SCANDALS SERIES:

- BRODY'S REDEMPTION
- FALLING FOR HER BOSS
- WITH THIS MAN

SECRET SANTA SERIES:

- SECRET SANTA
- SECRET SANTA II: A CHRISTMAS TO REMEMBER

MAKE ME A MATCH SERIES:

- ROMANCE RESET
- RULES OF ENGAGEMENT
- THE MATCHMAKER'S SECRET
- PERFECTLY MISMATCHED
- BY THE BOOK

CAROLINA COVE SERIES:

- SEASCAPES AND VEGAS MISTAKES
- SEASHELLS AND WEDDING BELLS
- SEA GLASS AND SECOND CHANCES
- SEA BLUE AND LOVING YOU
- SEA VIEW AND SOMETHING NEW

COMING SOON: (LINKS WILL BE UPDATED ASAP)

THE BLACKWELL BROTHERS SERIES:

- BABY BE MINE
- SECOND CHANCE WEDDING
- THE GETAWAY GUY
- OFF-LIMITS LOVE
- FLIRTING WITH FOREVER

About the Author

Kay Lyons always wanted to be a writer, ever since the age of seven or eight when she copied the pictures out of a Charlie Brown book and rewrote the story because she didn't like the plot. Through the years her stories have changed but one characteristic stayed true— they were all romances. Each and every one of her manuscripts included a love story.

Published in 2005 with Harlequin Enterprises, Kay's first release was a national bestseller. Kay has also been a HOLT Medallion, Book Buyers Best and RITA Award nominee. Look for her most recent novels with Kindred Spirits Publishing.

For more information regarding her work, please visit Kay at the following:

www.kaylyonsauthor.com

@KayLyonsAuthor (Twitter)

Kay Lyons Author (Facebook)

Author_Kay_Lyons (Instagram)

Kay Lyons, Author (Pinterest)

SIGN UP FOR KAY'S NEWSLETTER AND RECEIVE UPDATES ON NEW RELEASES, CONTESTS, PRE-RELEASE BOOK INFORMATION, EXCLUSIVES AND MORE!